TWO-FACED TRADE

The two gunmen reeled backward. Ned was able to get off a shot, but the bullet missed Gabe by more than a yard. Still firing, Gabe walked toward the two staggering gunmen, slamming more bullets into their already-shattered bodies. From the time Gabe charged back out of the alley, the shooting lasted only a few seconds, but the continuous roar of gunfire and the cries of the wounded made it seem much longer. Finally, the two Pinkertons fell in the middle of the street, stunned, mortally wounded, but not yet dead.

Gabe kicked the pistol out of Ned's hand. The other Pinkerton had already lost his. Gabe stood over them, a smoking pistol in each hand. "My only regret," he said, his voice bitter, "is that killing you won't bring back Ramon Garcia. Ramon was far too good a man to exchange for garbage like you."

He raised his pistols, pointing one at the head of each man. He saw the awareness of death in Ned's eyes. "Yeah," Gabe said softly. "In the face. Like Ramon."

His twin .44s roared together. Both Pinkertons were flung full length back onto the ground, their faces bloody pulp. They did not move again. Gabe looked down at what was left of them, then shook his head sadly. "Not worth the trade," he repeated. "Not worth it at all . . ."

LONG RIDER

THE SANTA FE RING

CLAY DAWSON

11

CHARTER BOOKS, NEW YORK

THE SANTA FE RING

A Charter Book/published by arrangement with
the author

PRINTING HISTORY
Charter edition/July 1990

ISBN: 1-55773-354-6

Charter Books are published by The Berkley Publishing Group,
200 Madison Avenue, New York, New York 10016.
The name "Charter" and the "C" logo are trademarks belonging
to Charter Communications, Inc.

PRINTED IN THE UNITED STATES OF AMERICA

10 9 8 7 6 5 4 3 2 1

CHAPTER ONE

Gabe first became aware of them as shadows. Shadows that were a bit too vivid, shadows that should not be where they were, shadows that moved.

He resisted an impulse to immediately quicken his horse's pace. Instead, he sat easily in the saddle, using his peripheral vision to track the shadows. He was sure nothing had been there half an hour earlier. They must have been waiting for him to enter the canyon. Or maybe they had been there all the time, and he had not noticed. His attention had been distracted when he'd ridden by those abandoned cliff dwellings. He'd let himself become lost in idle musings, wondering about the ancient Indians who had lived there, Indians who, instead of hunting for a living, as Gabe himself had done when he was growing up among the Lakota, had farmed, and chosen to live in settled communities. Hard to imagine. Indians—red men—living in houses, scratching the ground.

Perhaps the land hadn't given them much choice. It was so barren. The buffalo did not roam this far south. What would they eat? There were only light populations of deer and rabbit. Poor hunting. Since he'd come among the whites, Gabe had done considerable reading, searching for knowledge of the huge new world into which he'd been so precipitously thrown. Some of his readings of world history had told him that the early great agricultural societies had all grown up in arid lands: Egypt, Mesopotamia, the Valley of Mexico, where hunting was poor. Of course. Given the chance, who would exchange the joys of hunting for the misery of scratching in the ground like a hog? How lucky he himself had been, spending the first twenty years of his life riding with the People, hunting buffalo, raiding enemies. How sad he was that those days were over. But damned if he'd stoop to farming. Better to starve.

Those had been his thoughts when he'd ridden past those ancient structures. They'd been built into niches high up on the cliffs, their color blending into the cliffs themselves. The people who'd lived there had been penned like rats. Why not? When people began to accumulate possessions and to hold them in one place, other, more adventurous people, tended to want to take those possessions away.

None of which was enough to excuse his carelessness. He should have noticed that he was not alone, that others were near. He had originally thought that this particular route would take him far enough south of the Navajo reservation to avoid trouble with that bellicose tribe. Obviously not. And when a man got too close to Navajos, being careless could easily equal being dead.

They would of course take him for a white man. Which, he had to admit, he supposed he was, although he liked to think that his heart was all-Lakota. But, born of a white woman, with a white father whom he'd never known, he sure as hell looked one-hundred-percent white. He was a tall man with long sandy hair that hung down over his shoulders, and eyes so light a gray that they seemed almost without color. He was dressed as a white man, too, with a long linen duster covering his trousers and shirt. Too hot in this part of the world to wear the buffalo-skin coat he'd made out of the burnt remnants of his mother's tepee. Only the soft moccasins he wore, plus the length of his hair, said anything about his Lakota past. And what did it matter in the present situation? If those were indeed Navajos slipping through the nearby brush, it would not matter one little bit to them if he were white or if he were one-hundred-percent Lakota Sioux Indian. The Navajos were the enemy of every other people on the face of the earth. If they got him, he'd be dead meat.

Keeping the movement casual, Gabe urged his horse into a quicker walk, almost a trot. So far, he had seen no sign of movement ahead, just a few scattered shadows slipping through the rocks on either side, but considerably behind him. Perhaps he had been ahead of them all the time, or they had been slow about closing in.

Used to the vast plains of what the white man now called South Dakota, Gabe was a little uncomfortable in this broken, arid land, with its numerous buttes and jagged mountains. Eroded waterways, left over from flash floods, cut into the ground like wounds. A man could not see far here, not nearly far enough to spot his enemies before he was himself in immediate danger.

The shadows behind suddenly ceased being shadows. Gabe saw a man stand up about a hundred yards to his right, partly hidden by a boulder. A Navajo, all right. No mistaking the simple clothing, some of it white man's clothing, nor the headband holding the long black hair close to his big square head. He was aiming a rifle straight at Gabe.

Gabe instantly leaned forward and spurred his horse into a gallop. *Ka-wham!* A rifle shot echoed and re-echoed from the canyon walls, but the bullet missed, passing through the spot where Gabe had been sitting just before he'd spurred his horse forward.

Now more men were stepping into the opening behind him and to his sides. Gabe counted two or three, then put all his attention into riding as fast and as hard as he could. So far he'd seen no mounted men, so his plan was to simply outrun his attackers. The canyon opened up about a quarter of a mile ahead. Once he was in the open, they'd have little chance of catching him.

More shots sounded, more bullets whizzed around Gabe, but with his horse zigzagging around boulders and brush, he was a hard target to hit.

Until the man jumped him. Looking back over his shoulder, Gabe realized he had not paid enough attention to the ledge that overhung the trail a little ways ahead, so the man who'd been hiding there, lying flat and still on top of the ledge, had an easy time leaping onto Gabe from above.

Still, Gabe saw enough warning motion to twist in the saddle, avoiding the long knife that slashed at his back. But the man's weight, slamming into him hard, was enough to knock him from the saddle. They went down together, Gabe and the Navajo warrior, each man clutching the other desperately, the Navajo trying to get his knife into Gabe, Gabe trying just as hard to keep his skin unpunctured.

Gabe was much bigger than the Navajo. All that buffalo meat had helped him grow large and strong, and his size and strength now paid off. Twisting as he fell, he made sure that the Navajo was beneath him when they hit the ground, and as the air whooshed out of the attacker's lungs, Gabe first pinned the man's knife hand to the ground, then reached up under his linen duster, his fingers sliding along the side of the holster hidden beneath his armpit, the holster containing the big Colt .44.

But it was not the Colt he was after. Long ago he had sewn a knife sheath to the side of that holster, with the knife positioned inside it, butt downward. From long hours of practice, his fingers quickly found the knife handle, then pulled hard, freeing the knife from the snap catch that held it securely in place.

He slammed the point of the knife in just below the Navajo's ribs, angling the blade upward. The Navajo only grunted when the knife first went in, but when its tip found the underside of his heart, his body responded with a great leaping spasm, a last surge of strength that tried to save him from that terrible blade. But it was too late. A moment later the Navajo was dead.

Gabe leaped to his feet, knife in hand, his eyes searching the area for other hidden attackers. There seemed to be none. Perhaps the men behind and to the sides had been there merely to drive him toward this single hidden ambusher.

Gabe's horse, although startled by having its rider pulled from its back, was nevertheless standing in place just a few yards away, as Gabe had trained it to do. Stopping just long enough to wipe his knife blade partially clean on the dead Navajo's trousers, Gabe sheathed the knife and leaped up onto the horse's back. Barely in time. Men were closing in on him from both the left and the right. Guns crashed as he kicked his horse into a flat-out run, but once again all the shots missed.

The mouth of the canyon loomed ahead. He could only hope that no one else had gotten around in front of him. Not that he had much choice. To stay where he was, or to go back, meant death.

He reached the mouth of the canyon without further incident, and was beginning to breathe a little easier when he heard loud shouts behind him, closer than men on foot should have been. Glancing back over his shoulder, Gabe saw a dozen mounted Navajos pounding along after him. Obviously they'd had horses hidden somewhere but had decided to take him by stealth inside the canyon, where horses were less useful.

Nothing to do now but try to outrun them. The country ahead was fairly flat but fairly well covered with vegetation for western New Mexico: prickly pear, cholla cactus, small shrubs, and even grass and flowers. Beautiful land, but potentially deadly to a fleeing man. It would be easy for his horse to step into a hidden gopher hole.

Gabe's mount was a bigger, stronger animal than the horses the Navajos were riding, and for the next quarter of an hour he managed to pull slowly away from them. But his horse had been ridden hard for the past few days, with poor forage, and was quickly growing tired. If the men behind did not give up the chase soon, Gabe would have little choice but to stand and fight.

As he had expected, his pursuers did not give up. However, hope lay about a mile ahead, where the plain over which he was racing once again narrowed toward a canyon entrance. It wasn't much of a canyon, just a gash between low hills. The hills did not stretch very far in either direction, but at least the canyon entrance would give him a defensive position, a place from which he might be able to at least partially command the countryside behind him.

Pushing his horse as hard as he dared, Gabe managed to reach the canyon mouth about five hundred yards ahead of his pursuers. He immediately swung down from his horse, pulling his big Sharps carbine from its saddle scabbard as he dismounted. Making certain that the horse was screened from stray bullets, Gabe quickly took up a firing position near the top of a pile of rocks that partially hid the canyon entrance.

As always, there was a cartridge in the carbine's chamber. Gabe quickly raised the adjustable rear sight and set the crossbar for four hundred yards. He cranked back the big side hammer, then settled down to aim. Holding the leading Navajo right above the front bead sight, Gabe began squeezing the trigger. It was a very light and crisp trigger; he'd spent hours honing down the trigger and sear so that it would pull just right.

As usual, the rifle seemed to go off by itself. The heavy recoil slammed Gabe backward. He flipped the chamber open, which extracted the fired shell case, and was already sliding another of the big .50-caliber cartridges into the chamber even before the dense cloud of white smoke that had issued from the Sharps's muzzle had cleared enough for him to see the result of his shot.

The man he'd aimed at was down. The weight of the carbine's huge bullet had plucked him from the saddle almost as if he'd ridden into an overhanging tree limb. But the others were still coming on. Gabe got off another shot, this time bringing down a horse without hitting the rider.

Click, clank, clunk. Another round in the chamber. Years before, when Bridger had given him the Sharps, it had still used the old type of ammunition, a ball and a powder charge contained inside a waxed cartridge, as well as a percussion cap that had to be placed on an exterior nipple. Under that system the rifle had been accurate enough, but the rate of fire was too slow. As he crouched behind the rocks inside the canyon mouth, reloading, Gabe was very grateful that he'd had the rifle altered to take the newer metallic cartridges; his rate of fire was nearly tripled.

But now there was nothing more to shoot at. With one man killed and a horse and rider down, his Navajo pursuers were not foolish enough to continue riding straight on toward the murderous muzzle of the big Sharps. Instead, they had split off to the sides, disappearing from view. For a couple of minutes Gabe thought that they might have gone to ground, with the intention of sneaking up on him later, maybe after it grew dark.

Then he saw a flicker of motion off to his right, on high ground. A man on a horse! He noticed then how broken the walls of this canyon were, how other, smaller canyons ran into it from the sides, some of them behind where he was now. Obviously those canyons outflanked his position, and the Navajos, knowing the land better than he did, had realized it all along and were now circling around behind him.

Gabe had no choice but to remount his tired horse and get the hell out. He was almost too late. As Gabe rode by the mouth of one of the side canyons, men were already racing down it toward him. He had thrust the Sharps back into its saddle scabbard, and he now reached for his Winchester repeater, a better weapon for close-range fighting. He immediately dropped one man and forced the others to fall back. But in facing this one canyon, he had naturally turned his back on another leading in from the other direction. He only became aware of the men behind him when a bullet tore a groove in the flesh of his side, under his left arm.

Wincing, Gabe immediately spun his horse and charged the two men who'd gotten around behind him. He blew the first one out of the saddle and shot the second man's horse through the head. While the second rider was still in the air, having been pitched over his dying horse's head, Gabe sawed on the reins and pointed his horse further down the canyon. Shouts and wild yips of excitement coming from behind told him that his pursuers were hot on his heels.

His horse had gotten a little of its wind back during the brief fight among the canyons and was running fairly well, but Gabe knew that could not last for long. The animal had to play out soon. He'd have to find another place to make a stand. Hopefully a more impregnable place than the last.

Cliffs rose up ahead, nearly cutting off the far end of the canyon. As far as Gabe could see, there were no side canyons, no place to get around those cliffs. If he could find an accessible spot at the base . . .

But no, it wasn't to be. Somehow the Navajos had gotten more men around in front of him. He could see their dark shapes up on the cliffs: men with rifles, men wearing head-bands, men with dark Indian faces. He saw them raise their rifles, saw them aim down the canyon toward him, preparing to fire. Gabe jerked his horse to the side, frantically looking for some kind of cover, some place that would protect him from fire coming from both front and rear. There was nothing.

The rifles above roared. Gabe jigged his horse from side to side, looking for telltale dust spurts that would tell him how well those men up on the cliffs had him pinpointed.

But no bullets struck near him. And then he heard howls of pain and fear coming from the Navajos further down the canyon. Twisting in the saddle, Gabe saw that another of them had fallen. The others were milling about in confusion.

And then he noticed the bullets striking among them, kicking up dust, those that did not hit Navajo flesh. Looking back up at the cliffs, Gabe saw that those rifles were not aimed at him at all, but were firing at the men who'd been trying to kill him—the Navajos, who by now were pounding back down the canyon in full retreat. Somehow, he'd been rescued.

CHAPTER TWO

After the Navajos had disappeared pell-mell back down the canyon, an uneasy quiet fell over the battleground. For a while, nothing happened. Having no place to hide, Gabe had little choice but to sit his horse and wait. Finally, half a dozen riders came trotting around the edge of the cliff. They stopped about twenty yards away. It was clear to Gabe that they were studying him.

He studied them back. They were clearly Indians, but looked subtly different from the Navajos; more slender, more . . . how could he put it? More . . . peaceful? A strange word to use after the way they'd shot up the Navajos.

Gabe broke the silence. "Thank you for saving my life," he said in English. Most of the men facing him looked blank, then one muttered something to the others, who nodded. The one who'd spoken turned back toward Gabe. "Anyone whom the Navajo dogs attack, we help," he replied.

"They are enemies?" Gabe asked.

The man nodded. "Yes. Enemies of all civilized peoples."

Gabe looked somewhat puzzled. Enmity among Indians he understood. Most tribes were constantly at war with most other tribes, in a kind of unending guerrilla warfare, complete with raids, slaughters, and booty, a never-ending feud, broken by brief periods of peace . . . whenever the cost rose too high. But what did this comment about "civilized" mean?

He was wondering how to ask, when the man to whom he'd been speaking noticed Gabe sway a little in the saddle. Then the man saw the blood that had caked on the right side of Gabe's shirt. "You are wounded!"

Gabe shrugged and discovered that it hurt to shrug. "It's nothing . . . just a scratch," he replied, wondering if that were true. His side was beginning to hurt as though a cat were clawing at it.

Two men rode close, motioned toward his side. Gabe let them ease off his bloodied duster. He saw how they eyed the pistol and knife hidden beneath the duster. He slipped the shoulder harness off by himself. He was not fond of having others handle his weapons.

The men had to help pull his shirt free of his trousers and body. Drying blood had stuck the shirt to his skin; it hurt when they pulled the material away from the wound. However, he did not give the slightest sign of pain. From his earliest days he had been taught the tremendous, overriding importance of never showing pain.

The English speaker poked at the wound with a dirty finger. "You are right," he grunted. "Only a scratch. But it has lost much blood."

Someone else got out a strip of grubby cloth, which he tied around Gabe's torso, stanching the last of the blood. "You come with us," the English speaker said to Gabe. "We will take you to our city . . . fix you right."

City? Gabe merely nodded. He was tired; loss of blood did that to a man. And he wanted water. A Navajo bullet had passed through his canteen, saving his horse but wasting the water. However, he did not ask for water; that would show weakness, and a warrior never showed weakness.

It was only an hour's ride. Along the way the English speaker introduced himself as Juan Acoma. "Acoma is the name that the *padres*, the Spanish priests, gave to my family," he explained laconically. He did not explain where he had learned his English, and Gabe had better manners than to ask. Nor did he tell Gabe his Indian name. Juan was a medium-sized man, with a wiry build, a lean face dominated by a beaky nose, and neck-length black hair, held out of his eyes by a length of twisted red cloth that served as a headband. Gabe noticed that a magnificent piece of turquoise, mounted in silver, hung, suspended by a leather thong, around Juan's neck. While there were plenty of white men who would kill for a stone like that, Gabe doubted they would have an easy time taking that turquoise, or anything else, away from Juan Acoma.

The "city" turned out to be an Indian pueblo, housing a couple of hundred people. The entire pueblo was a collection of low, ocher adobe buildings clumped together in geometric confusion, rising from one story in front, to several stories further back. The ground-floor buildings had no doors or windows. Ladders leaning against the outside walls gave access to the roofs, which, at the lower levels, were the terraces of the next story above, each of which was set back from the story below. Gabe nodded. Good defensive thinking. If an enemy appeared, you just pulled up the ladders. No doors to break down, no windows to slip through.

Gabe was getting a little dizzy by the time they reached the pueblo. He didn't like it when he was separated from his horse and rifles, but he supposed he had little choice. He was helped up a ladder onto the roof of one of the houses, then led through the doorway of the next story. He entered a plain room, without anything inside that the white man might have thought of as furniture, mostly just skins on the floor, with wall niches for belongings.

An old woman was sitting cross-legged on a tattered deer hide. She looked up incuriously when the men brought Gabe into the room. One of the men said something to her, using a language of which Gabe understood not a word, although he spoke several Indian dialects. That was not unusual. There were hundreds of different Indian languages, some restricted to tribes with only a few hundred members. Gabe had smiled when he'd first read, years ago, in his mother's old Bible, the story of the Tower of Babel. That was a part of the white man's myth that Indians could easily understand.

The old woman got to her feet with some difficulty, then

came over to Gabe. She began to look more interested after she'd inspected his wound. She said something to the men in what Gabe took to be a sour tone, as if she were chiding them for their sloppy work. Turning toward an inside door, she called out, and a moment later two much younger women came into the room. They looked at Gabe curiously. He had his shirt off, and despite the blood and grime, he was a striking man. One tittered, holding her hand over her mouth, but the old woman said something to her in a sharp tone, and the girl looked abashed.

After what were obviously orders from the old woman, the younger ones left the room, returning a few minutes later with several pots and jugs. One contained water. The old woman began washing Gabe's wound, not very gently, but once again Gabe refused to show any signs of pain. When the wound was clean, Gabe looked down beneath his arm, and saw a long shallow tear, almost a blaze, where a bullet had torn the skin. Painful, but it should heal.

The pain began to subside after the old woman smeared a thick, rather ill smelling salve over the wound. She then bound it up by placing a piece of clean doeskin over the wound itself, holding it in place by wrapping one of the original dirty pieces of cloth around Gabe's torso. When the old lady had finished, she said something, and Gabe could have sworn he saw her almost smile.

One of the men did smile, and actually laughed. The old woman scowled at him. After she had turned and walked away, Juan told Gabe, "She said that you are to put your shirt back on. You put dangerous thoughts in the minds of the young women."

Gabe smiled. It was always better when men laughed together. "Tell her I thank her. And once again, I thank you, too, for driving off the Navajo."

"Ha!" Juan snorted. "Normal enough work for a civilized person . . . the driving away of wild dogs."

A look of fierce hatred and contempt had come over Juan's face. Gabe asked, "Your people, then, and the Navajo are old enemies?"

Juan shook his head. "No. The Navajo and their animal

cousins, the Apache, are only upstarts. It is we, the People, who are old. Old in this land, old here when the world was new. They came . . . they came. About the same time that the white men, the ones who call themselves Spaniards, came. What an evil day that was for my people.''

"I . . . have seen the same thing happen elsewhere,'' Gabe replied. "Far to the north. White men came . . . changed everything . . . destroyed . . .''

Juan snorted again. "Oh, the white men were a terrible disaster, but not as bad a disaster as the *Dineh*. That is what the Navajo call themselves. They and the Apache. They came to this land together many grandfathers ago. Two tribes of bandits who sometimes kill each other, and at all times kill whoever else they can find to kill. They must have been one people, originally, but they soon enough began killing one another. They came out of the north speaking much the same tongue, and almost immediately they saw—wild, starving dogs that they were—they saw our fields and our corn and squash and all the other good things that we had, that we had brought out of the earth with our labor. Almost immediately they began to raid, to steal, to kill. They took our crops, they destroyed our villages, they stole our young women to be their slaves or to kill slowly for their amusement. And while they were in awe of what we had, they showed contempt for it, too, destroying, always destroying. The Spaniard, with all his greed and evil ways, at least did not destroy our crops and fields and houses, but encouraged us to plant and build, even if he did take much of what we grew. Of course, we did have to please him from time to time by saying sacred words to his cold, distant, and very strange god. A little crazy, that one. However, one thing that we and the Spaniards had in common from the beginning was the necessity of fighting together against the Apache and the Navajo.''

The bitterness in Juan's voice was impossible to miss. "Yes,'' Gabe murmured. "I've heard of them, particularly the Apache.''

Juan laughed. "We gave them the names the white man calls them. In our language, Apache means 'enemy,' which they are. And the Navajo . . . we call them *Apache Na-baju*, which means 'enemy of cultivated fields.' Strangely enough, the Navajo eventually learned to plant trees and crops. I suppose they grew tired of starving when they could no longer steal as openly. But they have not grown tired of killing. In return, we kill them where we find them, like wild dogs. But we are different in our killing. We do not take pleasure in it. We do it only out of necessity.''

And then Gabe understood. That was the difference he had seen in the faces of the men who had rescued him. He had grown up among warriors much like the Apache and Navajo, warriors to whom fighting and killing was sport, was life itself, the only work fit for a man. But these pueblo people were farmers. He almost sneered, until he remembered that they had saved his hide. He satisfied himself by nodding to Juan.

Gabe stayed in the pueblo for several days, partly to let his wound heal well, partly out of curiosity. He had met few Indians who lived settled existences, who lived the way the white man had tried to make his own Lakota live. He found this fascinating, for, while the pueblo people were farmers, they were not at all like the white man. They were still Indians, and they saw the world around them as alive, bursting with personality, full of magical aspects with which they could communicate. His own Lakota had known the same spirits as the pueblo people—that which was alive in the sun, the wind, the earth, and the sky. But the Lakota had been aware of a sun that shines down on a moving people, of water that falls from the sky and grows the grass that fattens the buffalo, of a sky that is home to the hawk, a sky that moved with the people as they migrated over the face of the vast, dangerous, but motherly earth.

But to these neolithic farmers, the sun and rain was that which grew their crops, while the sky was the same sky they saw every day, stretching in an unmoving bowl over their unmoving village.

Gabe did not tell them about his Lakota life or his Lakota name. To these people Gabe's Lakota prairie pirates would be as hated a group as the savage local raiders who had caused them so much pain. He remembered then how the few plains tribes that practiced agriculture had often sided with the white man, guiding the soldiers to their hated common enemies, the nomadic hunters and raiders.

And now he understood more fully the impossibility of two such disparate ways of life coexisting. But however much his understanding improved, it did little to lessen the pain he felt at the loss of that old wild, free, adventurous life of roaming and raiding. It was time to leave these claustrophobic adobe houses and get back out under the open sky.

CHAPTER THREE

While in the pueblo, Gabe spent a good deal of his time practicing Spanish. He'd recently spent almost a year in Mexico, and with his knack for languages, had begun to speak Spanish fairly well. A wanderer by both nature and upbringing, Gabe had been curious about Mexico, curious about a people who had experienced almost as much trouble with the government and people of the United States as had his own people, the Lakota.

Eventually, Mexico had palled on Gabe. He felt constricted within its mountainous interior, oppressed by its old, established peasant way of life. He longed for open spaces again; plains, growing grass. He'd left Mexico several months ago, but the language had stayed with him.

The morning that Gabe left the pueblo, only Juan was there to say good-bye. Juan stood quietly for a while, watching Gabe cinch up the final straps that held his horse gear in place. Finally he spoke. "The others are not here as they should be," he said. "You have made them uneasy."

Gabe looked up, frowning. "Why? What is it that I have done?"

Juan shook his head. "Nothing. It is just that . . . that you do not seem to be . . . you do not seem to be quite a white man. You look like a white man, you speak the white man's language, but even then . . . there is something different about the way you use white man's words. That is what has made our people uneasy. That which they cannot fully understand."

Gabe nodded. "I hear what you say, and I . . ." He did not finish his sentence, but fell silent. His face was expressionless as he mounted. "Thank you again for saving my life, Juan Acoma. If I ever have the chance to repay that favor, I will do so."

He rode away, leaving Juan Acoma standing silently in front of his motionless, timeless pueblo, a man staring after that which he did not understand. Then Juan turned and walked back toward his house, not terribly perturbed. There was a great deal in this wonderful, mysterious world that a man would never be able to understand. And unlike a white man, he was not implacably driven to take the world to pieces, to divide it up, to analyze, and in doing so, destroy that very world. What was, was.

Gabe rode east from the pueblo, farther into New Mexico, toward the Rio Grande valley. He had heard that the land was good there, and as he rode, he thought about Juan's farewell comments. Not quite like a white man. He laughed bitterly. Not quite like anything—neither fish nor fowl, a man locked out, a man without a home. A man who had fought hard to keep his people free, who, like the rest, had failed, and was now cut off from the warmth of living among his own, the People. Cut off partly by the color of his skin.

After a few hours of riding, the land began to lose some of the sereness that had marked it near the pueblo, but it was still quite arid and without trees. However, there had been a little rain a few hours before, a quick summer thunderstorm, and the land had bloomed. The cholla and barrel cactus glistened with the moisture they had so efficiently sucked up from the temporarily wet earth. Grass had magically revived from its normal sere, blasted state, and although it was sparse, the grass nevertheless showed a soft green aliveness. There were a few delicate flowers poking up from the sandy soil, but most of the blossoms that had been brought out by this sudden gift of moisture had a leathery look. One species of plant, thrusting up near a clump of spiky Spanish bayonet, had waxy yellow flowers above what looked like bean pods. Gabe wondered if the pods could be eaten.

Most of the flora were new to Gabe, but the openness of the land was not; it stretched away from distant mountains to other distant mountains, and he felt an urge to kick his horse into a run so that he could feel the wind blow through his hair. As he rode across this dry New Mexico plain, he could not help remembering those other plains far to the north; greener plains, over which he had ridden as a boy, then later as a young warrior. Ridden with the People.

As for the early part of that life, the part he'd been too young to remember, he knew only what his mother had told him. His mother, Yellow Hair. He had an instant memory of her beautiful golden hair, before hard work and worry had changed it to a premature gray. He had another, later memory of that hair, streaked with blood. Her own blood.

When he was still little she'd told him how, way back when the white man was making his first inroads into the northern Great Plains, she and his father, attracted by the lure of gold, had entered the Black Hills with a party of other whites. The Black Hills, a special place, sacred to the Oglala and to their neighbors, the Cheyenne, was definitely off-limits to whites. It was an area fiercely protected by both these powerful tribes. Gabe's mother had told him many times how a war party of Oglala Bad Faces, a sub-grouping of the Lakota, the tribe the white men called the Sioux, had attacked the party, wiping out all but Gabe's mother. She had also told him, when he was old enough to understand, how she and his father, lying alone in their wagon that morning, had come together as man and woman and had conceived him. Conceived him only a few minutes before the Oglala struck.

Others among the Oglala had told him how his foster father, Little Wound, had been impressed by his mother's courage as she, the only survivor, had tried to brain Little Wound with an empty rifle. Little Wound had decided to spare her, had taken her for his woman, and after her son had been born, had raised Gabe as his own. Like most Lakota, Little Wound prized children, prized all new life. In a world where survival was so chancy, children were the tribe's entire future.

So Gabe had grown up an Oglala, not at all stigmatized
by his white skin the way a red child growing up among
the whites would have been stigmatized by his red skin.
Gabe's early values were Lakota values—the overriding
importance of courage, of never showing fear or pain, and
above all, a sense of belonging, of being part of, one with,
the tribe, the People.

Like any healthy growing boy given the opportunity,
Gabe had delighted in the joyful freedom of living out of
doors, of moving from place to place as the Oglala followed
their ambulatory general store, the buffalo. He learned to
hunt, to ride, to fight. He learned all the skills that later
prompted one U.S. Army general to describe the Plains
Indians as the ''Best light cavalry in the world.''

Now it all seemed like a dream, an insubstantial fantasy
fading away into the past. Even before Gabe's birth, the
Lakota were doomed. The white men, the hated Americans,
were pushing farther and farther into the West, bringing
with them that eternal enemy of all nomadic peoples—the
plow.

His mother, with her knowledge of the white man's ways,
and of his overwhelming material strength, had foreseen the
inevitable end of the Indians' way of life, its bloody end,
because the warriors of the plains would never give up their
land without fighting. Fighting to the death. She had images
of her son lying dead on some insignificant battlefield, insignificant to the white man, her son lying dead with a
soldier's bullet in his war-painted body.

So she had betrayed him. That was how Gabe himself
had thought of it at the time. But his mother had seen no
alternative. Aware that her son would never leave the Lakota
way of life on his own, Amelia Conrad, for that was her
white man's name, had taken advantage of an unexpected
situation to spirit Gabe away from the People. One day a
white man arrived at the Oglala camp, a famous mountain
man named Jim Bridger. Years before, Bridger had been
an ardent admirer of Amelia Conrad, had courted her. He
had long thought her dead, and now here she was, alive in

an Oglala village, with a white son who thought he was an Indian.

Bridger had begged Amelia to come away with him. She refused. She knew that if she went back to the white world, its religion-ridden, bigoted citizens would look on her as a pariah, a whore who had lain with a red man. She would be an outcast.

She convinced Bridger to kidnap her son, to take him away to an Army post, where he would learn the white man's way, where he would be out of danger.

It had not worked out quite that way. Penned into a life that he considered worse than death, without access to the wild, exciting openness of the plains, forced to perform white man's drudgery, the most insulting of all possible insults to a budding warrior, Gabe had fallen into a fight with a white officer, a Captain Price. As a result, he had spent three years in the guardhouse, a prisoner, completely shut away from the sun and sky and earth.

Then once again Jim Bridger appeared. Bridger got him out of the guardhouse by convincing the post commander that Gabe would make a fine scout. Gabe used this opportunity, this new freedom of movement, to go back to the People. Still bitter over his mother's apparent betrayal, it had taken Gabe awhile to forgive her. Then, finally understanding her motives, reconciled at last, he had settled back into tribal life. Gabe took an Oglala wife, Yellow Buckskin Girl, only to have both his wife and his mother murdered when the Army made a dawn surprise attack on the peacefully sleeping camp. Both his wife and his mother were killed before his eyes by that old enemy, the man he'd bested twice already, a man hungry for revenge, Captain Stanley Price.

Eager for his own revenge, Gabe decided to enter the white man's world, so that he could track down Stanley Price. The white man's road had taken him to Boston, where he met his mother's father, a wealthy Boston lawyer. With his grandfather's help, Gabe eventually found Stanley Price, whom he killed.

But the final revenge belonged to Price, or to men like

Price. The day of the free-roaming Indian, lord of the plains, was over. Gabe saw his people herded onto reservations, was himself denied access to the reservations because of his white skin, but would not have lived there, anyhow, in a place where the residents were not allowed to roam freely.

Both blessed and cursed by his white skin, Gabe had never stopped roaming. Yet he had always been touched by guilt that he, and he alone among the people with whom he'd once shared a life of wandering and hunting and combat, a life of courage and excitement, was the last survivor still free to do so.

As he rode across the New Mexico desert, half-lost in memory, Gabe touched the worn stock of his Sharps carbine. Jim Bridger had given him the carbine after he'd gotten him out of the guardhouse. It was strange how Bridger had appeared again and again in his life. Gabe would have liked to believe that Bridger was secretly his father. Unfortunately, his mother had been very definite in denying it. Gabe had compromised by taking his white name from Jim Bridger. Bridger had been known among his fellow mountain men as Old Gabe. Gabe had taken the name Young Gabe or later, just Gabe Conrad.

He'd had another name once, one he still used from time to time. When he was only fourteen years old, or when he'd had fourteen summers, as the Lakota would have put it, he'd made a difficult ride through a howling blizzard to warn the People of the approach of white soldiers. He had been remembered for that ride, and was still remembered among the few survivors of those glorious days. Hence the name, He of the Long Ride, best translated into English as Long Rider.

Still lost in thought, Gabe, Long Rider, sat his horse, unmoving, letting the animal head more or less as it wished. He rode with bitterness, remembering burned camps and bloody corpses, the corpses not only of warriors, but also of women and children. He remembered a war of extermination as the white man made the Great Plains safe for the plow.

It was in this frame of mind that he reached the little

Spanish settlement and saw what was happening there. Thinking about it later, it was undoubtedly the ugliness of those events, the way they awakened terrible memories, that made him do what he did.

CHAPTER FOUR

The village was not very large, just a dozen or so adobe buildings, along with a few wooden ones, clumped together in a broad valley near a grove of cottonwoods. While many of the buildings were low and square and flat roofed, they were not packed together as tightly as in an Indian pueblo. There were small yards and gardens, flourishing with chickens and corn and beans and squash, and there were corrals for horses.

It was not a rich place; poverty showed in many ways, yet this rather ragtag little town had a neat and broad town square, the plaza, bordered by houses, a cantina, and a *tienda*, or store.

It was from the cantina that the trouble had spread. As Gabe rode into town, the plaza was alive with approaching violence. Several horses were tied to the hitching rack in front of the cantina. They were cow ponies, loaded down with cowpunching gear: lariats, ponchos, chaps, brush jackets, and rifles. The horses' owners, five heavily armed cowpunchers, were wandering up and down in front of the cantina, obviously, from their raucous, drunken voices, having overimbibed inside.

Gabe immediately recognized the nasal Texas twang that dominated the cowhands' speech, and from that alone he knew that things were not good. He was right. A shot rang out from inside the cantina. A moment later another cowhand came out into the plaza, waving a pistol, whooping and hollering. "Goddamn it, boys!" he howled. "Let's teach these here greasers just how fine us Texans can shoot.''

His companions cheered drunkenly. Raising his pistol, the cowhand put a bullet into the middle of the worn board sign that hung over the door of the store. His next bullet went through the store's single glass window. The other cowhands, laughing, also began shooting at the window, obviously not caring whether or not there might be someone inside. Finally, the proprietor, a man in his sixties, came running out through the doorway, screaming maledictions. He was a brave man, Gabe thought, to face these drunken Texans, men whose mouths were far larger than their brains.

The cowboy who'd shot first decided to have a little fun with the store owner. "Well, lookee, boys," he shouted, laughing. "A greaser tryin' to act like a man."

He'd been reloading his pistol, and now he sent a bullet into the dirt near the store owner's feet. The storekeeper jumped back, which made all the cowhands laugh. The cowboy shot again, but this time the old man did not move, but stood his ground, staring with contempt at the Texan. The cowhand fired another shot. The old man still did not move, but, speaking softly and clearly, uttered the most dreadful swear word he could think of. "*¡Tejano!*" he hissed. "Texan!"

A low growl passed among the Texans. Normally such courage might have impressed them, but not from the store-keeper, not from a Latin. "Why . . . you fucking Mes'kin," the cowhand who'd started it all snarled, and shot the old man through the leg.

The storekeeper went down hard, grunting from the impact of the bullet, but otherwise not crying out. He lay on the ground, his eyes glazed with pain and shock, but he was still defiant, he still met the eyes of the man who'd shot him.

This continued defiance might have earned him another bullet; Texas had, with great cruelty, already wiped its own borders free of Mexicans, blacks, and Indians. This particular Texan was quite willing to start the same chore all over again here in New Mexico, but as he was raising his pistol a young woman ran from inside the store. "*¡Abuelo!*" she cried out, then fell to her knees next to the old man.

The sneer on the gunman's face turned to a leer. "Well, well, lookee here, boys," he said in his whining drawl. "They got some good-lookin' pussy in this dump, after all."

The other Texans hooted similar sentiments, slapping their thighs in merriment. The girl remained bent over her grandfather, trying to comfort him, while the old man did his best to push her away, begging her to get out of there quickly, before the men hurt her, too.

She refused. It was already too late. The man who'd shot the girl's grandfather jerked her to her feet. "Come on, Conchita," he said, grinning at her. "Let's you an' me have us a little fun."

The girl, anxious to break free, struggled against his grip. He spun her partway around, and when she was off balance, grabbed the front of her blouse, which tore, baring most of her breasts. They were very lovely breasts. The other cowhands cheered and clapped as the girl tried to cover her nudity.

Then the cowhand was on her again, a bit clumsily, since he still held his pistol in his right hand. As he grabbed the girl's arm, she suddenly spit in his face. He was so surprised that he let her break free again. She backed against the adobe wall of the store, breathing hard, almost sobbing, her face reflecting fear, anger, humiliation, and hatred.

The cowhand raised his left hand and wiped at the spittle that was running down one cheek. "Why, you little greaser bitch," he snarled.

He half raised his revolver. Would he have shot the girl? No one was to find out, because at the moment a boy came bursting out of the store's doorway, a pick handle in his hand, screaming at the cowhand to leave his sister alone. The boy was young, perhaps no more than thirteen or fourteen, but that was not enough to stop the cowhand. Spinning, he shot the boy through the chest.

The boy fell the way a dead man falls, uttering not a word, not a move after he hit the ground. For a second or two, after the roar of the shot had died away, there was not another sound in the plaza; an awful silence froze everyone in place.

Then the girl screamed, a terrible, piercing scream, a blend of horror and hatred, then, dodging past the cowhand, she ran to her dead brother. She fell on the body, clutching it to her, while the old man, despite his wounded leg, began dragging himself toward the gunman, a look of such hatred and violence on his face that the gunman fell back a step, alarmed by the very vehemence of that look.

He might have shot the old man again, added another victim to his score, had not a new force entered the melee, for it was a melee now, with people screaming and shouting from doorways, while the cowhands, either shaken or gleeful over what had happened—it was hard to tell—began pegging shots into walls and windows.

Gabe had been sitting his horse quietly all this time, telling himself that only a fool involved himself in other people's troubles. But from the start of the violence, images had been forming in his mind, old images. The cowhands, the aggressors, were white. Loud and white and arrogant. Their victims had darker skin and long, straight black hair like the Lakota, like his own people. And the faces . . . from centuries of mixing their Spanish blood with the blood of the New World, the inhabitants of this little village had features not at all unlike the features of the People.

As Gabe's senses took in these various bits and pieces of information, his memory rebuilt horrific images of burning camps, of slaughtered men, women, and children, of men like these Texans firing into helpless, already-wounded bodies.

Something snapped inside Gabe. He let out a wild, high-pitched yell, the war cry of the Lakota, and suddenly his Winchester was in his hands and his heels were thudding against the ribs of his horse, jolting it into a run.

There was already a shell in the Winchester's chamber. Gabe cranked back the hammer and raised the rifle to his shoulder. The man who'd shot both the old man and the boy had spun around at the sound of Gabe's war cry. For a moment he was confused. He'd expected to see an Indian thundering down on him, but saw instead a white man.

This moment of hesitation gave Gabe plenty of time to put a bullet through the man's chest, knocking him over backward. Now there was no stopping; the four surviving cowhands were scattering before Gabe's wild charge, clawing for their pistols. Gabe shot one man through the head as he rode through the pack. Two or three shots were fired after him, but by then he was all the way through the plaza, and a moment later he had disappeared around the corner of a building.

"Gawd Dayum!" one of the Texans shouted, looking around disbelievingly at his two dead companions. Then his confusion turned to anger. "Let's git after him, boys," he shouted to the two others, " 'fore he gits away!"

But Gabe had no intention of getting away. Far from it. As the Texans were running for their horses, they were stopped by the thunder of hoofbeats approaching fast from the direction in which Gabe had disappeared. A moment later Gabe burst out from behind the corner of the same building, riding low on his horse's back, his Winchester spitting fire and lead.

One man went down immediately. Another got off a shot that missed Gabe. Leaning low from his saddle, Gabe clubbed the man to the ground with his rifle barrel.

But as he went down, the cowboy grabbed hold of the rifle, tearing it from Gabe's grasp. The only cowboy still on his feet, seeing his chance, gave up trying to hide behind his horse, and came out shooting. Gabe jinked his horse to one side, avoiding the bullets, then, reaching beneath his duster with his left hand, brought out his .44 and shot the man in the throat.

While that man was still falling, Gabe turned his attention to the man who'd grabbed his rifle barrel. The rifle had fallen to the ground, and the cowhand, dazed by the blow to his head, was scrambling for it. Gabe took careful aim and shot him through the forehead.

With the killing rage still in him, Gabe pirouetted his horse, pistol in hand, looking for more men to kill. But of his original five opponents, all were now dead or dying, lying on the ground not far from where the old man and the boy lay. The peaceful plaza had been turned into a killing ground.

The blood lust slowly faded from Gabe. Now was the time for cool thought, for making certain that no more danger threatened. Were there more cowhands in the town? Would the townspeople themselves turn against him?

But there was no sign of further danger. The five dead cowhands were still the only gringos in sight. And the local population, rather than showing hostility, were showing caution, keeping out of sight. Gabe noticed a few faces at windows or doorways, but other than the dead and wounded and the girl, the plaza was empty.

Gabe quickly reloaded his pistol, then put it away into its shoulder rig. "*¡Venga!*" he called out in Spanish. "Come out here and help these people."

For a few seconds, nothing happened, then a middle-aged woman came out of a doorway and walked quickly over to the girl, who was still lying over her brother's body. She pulled the girl aside, made a quick examination of the boy, shook her head bitterly, then moved over to the old man, who had by now passed out. She took his hand and stroked it tenderly.

Now more people were coming out into the open. Gabe, in an effort to look less threatening, dismounted, picked up his Winchester, and thrust it back into its saddle scabbard. Looking around at the growing crowd, he saw that there was still fear in their eyes. "Don't be afraid," he told them in Spanish. "It's all over now."

One of the onlookers, an old man with a short white beard, detached himself from the others and came over to stand facing Gabe. He met Gabe's eyes, and Gabe saw ineffable sadness in those dark old eyes. "No, *señor*," the old man said sorrowfully. "It is not over at all. Quite the contrary. It has barely started."

CHAPTER FIVE

The plaza was a scene of continuing confusion. Women were wailing over the corpse of the boy. A group of men and women were carrying the old man into a house. Others gathered about the bodies of the dead Texans, looking down with hatred at the men who had violated their town.

The old man with the beard motioned for Gabe to follow him. He led the way into one of the town's larger houses. It was quite cool inside; the house's thick adobe walls kept out the heat of the sun. The room they entered had white-washed walls, with a floor of rough handmade tiles. Dark beams crossed overhead from wall to wall. The furniture—there was not much of it—was made of heavy, dark wood.

As the two men entered the house, a stout, middle-aged woman came out of another room to meet them. That other room appeared to be a kitchen; Gabe was aware of the smell of food coming from that direction, coming from the woman herself. It reminded him that he was very hungry. "Maria," the old man said, "please bring us something to eat. And to drink."

The woman nodded silently, then disappeared back into the kitchen. The old man motioned toward a table and two chairs. "Let us sit and talk," he said.

They sat down on opposite sides of the table. Neither man said anything for a while, but took time to study the other. They were still sitting silently when the woman reappeared carrying a large tray. She quickly covered the table with plates full of tortillas, chiles, and cooked meat. Then she placed a bottle on the table, with a glass for each man. Don Javier uncorked the bottle, and was about to fill Gabe's glass, but Gabe stopped him. He could smell alcohol. "I do not drink," he said.

Don Javier looked at Gabe in amazement, as if unable to believe that a grown man did not drink. But he overcame his surprise. "Coffee, then?" the old man asked.

"I am not at all thirsty. But the food . . ."

Don Javier gestured toward the plates, then poured himself a glass of what looked like wine. Gabe addressed himself to the food, and while he was helping himself to tortillas and meat, he studied the old man. He liked the way he looked, liked the dignity of him. He liked the food, too; the meat was in a rich sauce, and the chiles bit pleasantly. "What did you mean out there in the plaza?" Gabe finally asked, after his first mouthful. "When you told me that something was only starting."

The old man sighed. "I'm afraid that I was a bit dramatic, but then, it was a dramatic moment, wasn't it? Six dead, another wounded, people screaming and cursing, gunsmoke in the air."

The old man smiled, the first smile Gabe had seen from him. A smile that suggested that the old man was not personally adverse to gunsmoke and bodies. "Let me introduce myself," he said. "My name is Javier Solis. I . . . have some influence here."

Now Gabe smiled. "I have no doubt of that, Don Javier. But . . . you were going to explain to me what you said in the plaza."

Don Javier's face turned grim again. He took a sip of his wine. "Ah, yes. It embarrasses me, what I'm about to tell you. No one likes to explain why they live in fear. Of course, we've always lived in some kind of fear here in New Mexico; fear of the Apaches and Navajos, and at one time even of the Comanches, before they moved farther to the east. Those fears were all real, are still real, and we've lost many people. However, we fought both the fear and the Indians, met them face-to-face. We fought them standing together, with the blessings of our government. However, since the war between the United States and Mexico . . . "

Gabe nodded. This land, once belonging to Spain, and later to Mexico, had become part of the United States a generation before, taken by force of arms, along with California, Arizona, Nevada, and parts of Colorado. It was a vast area, sparsely settled before the Americans came, but beginning to fill up now.

"They call us Mexicans," Don Javier said, obviously musing. "We do not call ourselves that. We are Spanish. We came to New Mexico two hundred years before Old Mexico gained its independence from Spain. And precious little we ever got from Mexico, with its endless revolutions and governmental corruption. How we languished here, cut off from the outside world, but we endured. For more than two hundred fifty years we have remained something that is . . . of ourselves. Complete. Until the gringos . . . until the Americans came."

Gabe nodded. "Don Javier," he said, "you paint a picture of which I am well aware."

The old man looked at him with surprise. "I think that perhaps you genuinely understand," he said. "What you did out there today . . . "

"Yes. That which you say has only just started," Gabe finished for him, probing.

"Ah . . . yes. You see, *señor* . . ."

"Conrad. My name is Gabe Conrad. Are you going to tell me that the law will go after you for the killing of men who were in the act of killing innocent people?"

Don Javier laughed bitterly. "Well, Señor Conrad, we may be guaranteed rights by your government, but those rights are very difficult to claim . . . unless you're an Anglo. Our lands and property are stolen with impunity, and we are despised, we are even murdered . . . because we are of a different culture."

Gabe nodded. "As I said . . . I'm hardly surprised."

He thought of what was happening to his own people, the Lakota, with crooked government agents stealing the food and supplies that had been promised them in exchange for their stolen land. And now even more land was being stolen, in violation of solemn treaties.

Don Javier seemed a little confused again, as if Gabe were some strange species he was having trouble identifying. "Who are you, Señor Conrad?" he asked.

Gabe looked away. "Just a man . . . passing through."

"Ah, yes. Those men you killed today. They were just passing through, too. They pass through every year."

Gabe said nothing, but raised his eyebrows in a silent question.

"They work for a rancher, John Slaughter," Don Javier continued. "Slaughter has large ranches in Texas, and ranches further north of here. Every year he drives his herds through this part of New Mexico. Herds that magically grow larger as they move. Señor Slaughter has a habit of sweeping up any cattle he finds along his route, and of joining those cattle to his herds . . . even if those cattle belong to other men. And if those other men complain . . . pow! He has them shot. Especially if they are what men like Señor Slaughter call 'Mes'kins.' Señor Slaughter is a loyal Texan, and Texans believe that New Mexico should be a part of Texas. We here in New Mexico feel differently. But Señor Slaughter has the guns, and he has the law on his side. So we endure."

"And this just goes on and on?" Gabe asked, a little acerbically.

Don Javier smiled, somewhat coldly. "You mean, of course, that we do not fight back. That is not quite true, Señor Conrad. We are not a docile people. But we have the weight of a huge country against us. Last year, two men of our town . . . complained, about what was happening. They shot three of Slaughter's men, after those men had shot up our village pretty much as it was shot up today. But that was not the end of it. The next day more Slaughter men came, twenty of them, accompanied by a man who called himself a marshal. They hung our two young men from a tree, over in our own cottonwood grove. Their wives and mothers cut them down after they were dead. Strangled. A horrible way to die. We are a small village, Señor Conrad.

We cannot afford to keep losing our young men. Who would feed the women and children? So, as I have said, we endure. But today, Señor Conrad, you have killed five of John Slaughter's men. Killed them here in our village. I am happy that you killed them, Señor Conrad; they needed killing. But Slaughter will want to, as he might say, 'even the books.' By spilling our blood.''

Gabe nodded. ''And what will you do?''

''We will fight back, of course. But we will lose. There will be too many of them. They will shoot some of us, hang a few more.''

Gabe was beginning to grow angry. He hated injustice. Injustice was a word, a concept, that he had learned from his white grandfather, and when faced with it he always responded with anger. It made him even angrier when faced with the calm fatalism of this old man, Don Javier. If Don Javier had whined or whimpered, Gabe would have despised him. The society in which he had been raised, Lakota society, despised cowardice and whining above all else. But to see a village bullied and butchered by a bunch of ignorant cowhands . . .

Gabe stood up. ''Those men will not come here to harm you, Don Javier. After all, you are not to blame.''

Don Javier shrugged. ''True. But . . . how will they know that?''

Gabe looked him straight in the eye. ''Because I'll tell them so.''

CHAPTER SIX

"You know that you don't have to do this thing," Don Javier said.

"I know," Gabe replied. "But I choose to."

He was not certain that it was completely true. Once again he wondered if somehow the old man, intent on saving his village, had manipulated him into doing this rather . . . insane thing. He decided that it didn't matter. What he was about to do had a rightness to it; it was the true path of a warrior. The strong must always protect the weak.

He turned away from Don Javier and watched the village men lash the last of the dead Texans across the back of the man's horse. The horse, alarmed by the smell of blood and the growing stench of corruption, was complaining mightily, but to no avail. Don Javier's people were obviously very good with horses.

They were using the Texans' own animals, with each Texan draped across the saddle that had carried him into town. The men's gear was in place, all of it, including the guns with which they had shot up the village. Both Gabe and Don Javier were adamant that nothing that had belonged to the dead men turn up missing.

Finally, it was done. A young man brought Gabe's horse. "A fine animal, *señor*," he said, stroking the horse's flank. Gabe nodded, then turned back toward Don Javier. He pointed to the bodies. "They'll be smelling pretty bad by the time I get them there. You say it's about a four-hour ride?"

"Yes. You'll know the place by the big cattle herds outside town. That's been Slaughter's headquarters for the last two weeks, although he's not there at the moment. We've heard that he's in Santa Fe, talking to the territorial governor.''

Don Javier's nose wrinkled, as if he were smelling something bad. "The governor," he murmured. "Another very corrupt man sent to us by that father of all corruption, the president.''

Gabe refused to be drawn into this new conversational tack. He despised politics and politicians, and refused to waste words on either. "I'll be going, then," he told the old man.

Don Javier blinked. For just a moment his resolve seemed to waver, and Gabe was afraid that the old man would break down, would beg him not to go, and in so doing would damage Gabe's own resolve. But Don Javier quickly mastered his emotions. "*Vaya con Dios*," he said softly, then abruptly turned away.

Gabe walked to his horse, and then was aware that someone was walking beside him. He turned. It was the girl who's brother had been killed. He'd learned that her name was Elena. "*Señor*," she said hesitantly. "*Por favor . . . un momento?*"

He stopped walking and turned toward her. He was considerably taller, and when he met her gaze, he found himself looking down into a pair of large, dark eyes, eyes of a surpassing softness. He realized just how pretty the girl was; it was not only the big eyes, but also the full lips, the small straight nose, and skin the color of a dusky rose. She was dressed like most of the other women, wearing a full skirt that came down a little past her knees and a white blouse cut low, draping off her shoulders. The blouse showed a considerable amount of impressive cleavage, and Gabe remembered the glimpse he'd caught of the girl's breasts when the cowhand had torn away the front of her blouse. Elena was without doubt a very lovely girl, and quite young, no more than seventeen or eighteen years old.

"*Señor*," she said, "I want to thank you for what you did for us, for all of us."

He nodded, but said nothing, aware that the girl's presence disturbed him. Why? Perhaps because it had been so long since he'd had a woman, and this one was very desirable. But perhaps there was more to it than simple abstinence; perhaps it had to do with this particular girl, with the way she was looking at him. There was an intensity in her gaze, and she was looking into his eyes with an unsettling directness. "*Señor*," she said, her voice suddenly tense, fierce, "kill those sons of pigs. Kill as many of them as you can."

Surprise kept Gabe from answering. If this had been a Lakota girl, he would have been less surprised, for Lakota women sent their men off to war with the women's blood cries ringing in their ears. This girl was certainly not a Lakota, but neither was she like the meek, scheming white women of whom he'd seen way too many over the past few years. Elena quickened his blood. Looking into those big dark eyes, hot now with passion, he suspected that she would not resist, at least not for long, if he took her by the hand and led her to some private place where they would be able to fulfill that passion. He could feel her swaying toward him, all hot blood and vengeance.

Gabe pulled back. To touch a woman before a fight was bad medicine. "I promise you, I'll do whatever I have to do," he told her, then mounted his horse.

He thought he saw a brief flash of disappointment in her eyes, but then she nodded and stepped back, stern faced. "Go with God," she told him in Spanish, "I will pray for you, *señor*. Pray to the Virgin."

Gabe nodded. He took hold of the lead rope that tied together the horses carrying the bodies, then nudged his own horse into a walk. There were a number of people present, but no one cheered. All wore solemn faces, for every man and woman knew that this stranger was on their behalf, going to an almost certain death. It was not a time for cheering.

For a few minutes the other horses, with their gruesome

load, tried to hold back, but Gabe pulled firmly on the lead
rope, and they began to quiet down. He led his gruesome
little cavalcade up into a range of hills. Within half an hour
he could no longer see the village, which was good; the
village had been a place of too many confusing emotions.
It happened often; villages that were fixed, that did not
move, that could not be packed up at a few hours' notice
were usually like that—bad feelings stuck to them.

It was good to be out in the open again, riding toward
battle. War, the hunt, the fellowship of one's fellow warriors, the closeness of the tribe, all these were a warrior's
true business. He had lain in Don Javier's house most of
the night on a sagging bed made of rope, thinking. For far
too long he'd been wandering aimlessly, not caring whether
he lived or died, observing without participating, devoid of
a sense of belonging, cut off from human warmth. Now he
had a chance to do something worthwhile, to do something
for a people, even if they were not his own people, his own
defeated, dying people. He would be doing a man's work
today even if it killed him. Which it very easily might.

He felt a flash of anger toward himself. He knew that a
man who rides into battle expecting only to die is merely
throwing his life away. True, a man must always be ready
to die, must be indifferent to the thought of death, but he
must also be ready to survive, to let his enemies do the
dying.

Of course, it helped if a man had something to live for.
An image of Elena flashed through Gabe's mind; the big
dark eyes, the softness of her skin, her obvious courage.
She was life. He would hold her in his thoughts, make of
her—someone almost unknown to him—a pillar on which
to fasten his desire to live.

Steadied, Gabe rode on. Don Javier had said that the
town where he would find most of the cowhands lay four
hours away. It was now ten in the morning. There was no
hurry. It would be better to arrive just before dark, when
men are tired, when the approaching darkness would be
there to provide a haven for a solitary, hunted man.

Gabe rode for another three hours. Several miles short

of the town, he led the horses a little further up into the hills, to a high point from which he could see most of the surrounding countryside. Behind him, to the east, lay high, rugged mountains, the Sangre de Cristo range. The Blood of Christ. Gabe smiled. The old Spaniards who had settled this land had used very colorful names to describe it. They must love it very much.

How cluttered his thoughts were! How fragmented his concentration! Now was the time to prepare for what lay ahead. Gabe dismounted, then tied all the horses securely to some of the smallish pine trees that grew on the hilltop. He walked around for a few minutes, feeling for the spirit of this hilltop, whether it was a good spirit or a harmful spirit.

Finally, satisfied that this was a good place, a place of power, he took off his long linen duster and carefully folded it. Then he opened his saddlebags and took out a cartridge belt and pistol, which he fastened around his waist. The pistol, a Colt .44–40, identical to the one holstered beneath his right arm, rested high on his right hip, butt forward, cavalry style, although there was nothing military about the cut-down holster that left all of the pistol's butt and part of the trigger guard bare.

He then untied his bedroll from behind the saddle. Laying it on the ground, he unrolled it. Inside was a heavy coat made of buffalo hide. Draping the coat over a rock, he rolled the duster inside the bedroll and put it back where it belonged, behind the saddle.

He turned back toward the rock. With the coat draped over it, he could clearly see the painted thunderbird that spread its wings over the coat's shoulders and back. *Wakinyan*, the Winged God, his protector, who had appeared to him so many years ago, when as a young man he had sought a vision. For days he had fasted and chanted alone on a mountaintop, until finally the Winged One had come, had wrapped its protecting wings around his body.

Wakinyan. His mother, impressed by the force and depth of her son's vision, had painted the thunderbird figure onto the brand-new tepee cover she'd been making. The tepee that had been burned only a few days later, when the white soldiers had attacked. That terrible day when Captain Stanley Price had murdered both Gabe's mother and his wife.

All that had been left of the tepee cover was a smoldering segment that contained the thunderbird painting. Gabe had salvaged the scorched leather, and later had fashioned it into the coat that now lay draped over the rock. The colors had faded many times, but each time he had renewed them. They glowed for him now.

Gabe picked up the coat and put it on. As usual, the moment the wings of *Wakinyan* settled across his shoulders, as they had during his vision, he felt a sense of power, of being protected, of being whole, cleansed.

The coat was a pleasant weight; the afternoon had begun to grow chilly. Gabe walked across the hilltop to a place that he had already selected as a special place. He sat down, cross-legged, stilling his mind, opening himself.

The view was awesome; he could see for miles. Behind him, the afternoon sun was shining against the peaks of the Sangre de Cristo. A little snow remained at the higher elevations; the sun made the snow gleam. The mountains radiated strength.

Gabe turned away from the mountains, felt their power flowing through him, pressing down toward the land below. There were several valleys directly below his hilltop. This was a dry land, but bright patches of green showed wherever there was water. Crops, grass, trees. In this land, availability of water meant life or death. Naturally, men fought over what water there was. Men always fought.

The moment came when it was time to go; the shadows were growing long. Gabe stood up, and the moment he reached his full height, he heard a loud, harsh cry coming from above. He looked up. An eagle was soaring past, not more than twenty feet above his head. The eagle screamed again and hovered over him. Gabe had a moment to look into its fierce, unblinking eyes. He felt a sudden elation, felt new strength surge through his body. *Wakinyan* had spoken.

Collecting the horses, Gabe rode back down the mountain. Half an hour later the town lay a ten-minute ride below him. He found a good vantage point on a hilltop and stopped for a few minutes, studying the town's layout. It was a bigger town than Don Javier's little village, which might be helpful. A man could lose himself in such a town.

Gabe took a pair of binoculars from his saddlebag and spent several moments studying and memorizing the town's various features: where the larger buildings were, the livery stable, the saloon, the bank. This particular town was less Spanish, more Anglo, with many false-fronted wooden buildings.

Gabe noticed that a network of narrow, curved alleyways snaked behind the buildings that lay on the town's two main streets. Potentially useful information. A plan began to form inside his head.

Gabe put the binoculars away, and was ready to ride again, but a glow from behind made him turn in the saddle. The last of the sun was painting the highest peaks of the Sangre de Cristo a deep red. The Blood of Christ. Fitting. This could indeed be a night of blood. Perhaps his own blood. Gabe laughed. As the Lakota were fond of saying, only the rocks live forever.

He kicked his horse into a walk. The other horses followed patiently. Halfway down the hill, he looked back again at the glory that the setting sun had made of the mountain peaks. Let death touch whom it wished—this was a beautiful day for dying.

CHAPTER SEVEN

It was dusk by the time Gabe rode into town, but there was still enough light for those with a view of the main street to see the grim nature of the cargo the horses trailing behind him were carrying. Naturally, men began to gather. "Hey! That's Pete!" a cowhand called out, recognizing one of the bodies.

Gabe stopped right in the center of town, where the buildings were the thickest. That was part of his plan.

"Who did it, mister?" a man asked him. "Injuns?"

Gabe did not answer directly. "Is there someone here representing the Slaughter outfit?" he asked.

"Yeah. Don Harrison. He's the foreman of the local work crews."

"Get him."

A man went away to fetch Harrison. Gabe remained sitting his horse. He had ridden into town with his Winchester held in his right hand, the barrel slanting upward, the butt resting on his right thigh. He sat without moving, only his eyes active, scanning the men who had gathered around him. So far, so good; it was an unthreatening crowd, just a few cowhands, some barflies who'd come out of the saloon a few doors down to find out what all the excitement was about, and some townspeople—the merchant and teacher class who lived off the real workers.

The man who'd gone to fetch the foreman returned with a medium-sized, work-hardened man around forty years old. His dusty, trail-worn clothing suggested that he was a working foreman, and not the kind of boss who sat back and let others do all the sweating. He cast a quick glance in the direction of the bodies, then looked up at Gabe. "What's all this, mister?" he asked. His voice was not friendly.

"Are you John Slaughter's foreman?" Gabe asked back.

"Yeah. One of 'em. Name's Harrison. Who the hell are you?"

Gabe ignored the question, then pointed toward the corpses. "Those dead men are Slaughter hands."

Harrison's eyes never blinked, remained partially hooded. "I can see that. I recognize a couple. Who killed 'em."

"I did."

A murmur swept through the crowd. Harrison's eyes still didn't blink; he stood unmoving, although his eyes grew even colder. "I think you got some explainin' to do, mister."

Gabe let a moment pass, and while he waited, he studied the other cowhands. He'd counted four so far, but there was a chance others would head this way soon, alerted by the news. "I shot them after they'd shot an old man, killed a boy, and molested a girl. They were shooting back."

Harrison chewed his lip. "That's not good enough, mister. Nobody kills my men. No matter what they do."

Gabe waved his rifle barrel in the direction of the bodies. "Obviously, you're wrong. And so were they. They were terrorizing a town full of peaceful people. Los Robles. And I'll tell you this now. I'll say it once and only once. Any other man who does the same will end up just as dead."

Harrison stood tensely, staring up at Gabe, but he made no immediate move. He's smart, Gabe thought. He sees my rifle, knows he'll go down first.

But one of the watching cowhands was not quite as cautious as his foreman. "You mean," he bellowed incredulously, "that you killed Pete an' the others just for shootin' up a town full o' *greasers*?"

The man's accent pegged him as a Texan. Gabe had met many Texas gunmen who bragged about killing this or that many men, "not includin' Meskins or injuns." Obviously

Gabe was facing such a man now. "Why, you back-shootin' bucket o' shit . . ." the Texan snarled, reaching for his pistol.

Gabe swung the barrel of his rifle, pulled back the hammer, and shot the cowhand through the shoulder. The cowhand spun to one side, the pistol falling from nerveless fingers, then he began to roll on the ground, howling with pain. He was still rolling as Gabe levered another round into the Winchester's chamber. He swept the barrel over the assembled crowd. "He was lucky," Gabe said coldly. "But I'll kill the next man who goes for a gun."

"I do think you would," Harrison replied just as coldly, but he was careful to make no overtly hostile moves. One of the cowhands shifted his weight a little. "Hold it, Joe!" Harrison said sharply. "He's got the drop on us . . . for the moment."

"Just keep remembering that," Gabe said. He jerked his head toward the corpses. His rifle barrel never wavered. "There's your dead," he said flatly. "All their gear is with them. Take care of them as you see fit . . . as long as you understand a couple of things: They got what they deserved. And anybody else who tries shooting up Los Robles, or any other town in these parts, will end up the same as them . . . dead."

Harrison shook his head. "It's you that's the dead man, mister," he said softly. "You're gonna go down, either full o'lead, or swingin' at the end of a rope. Jus' so's you understand."

"I don't think so," Gabe replied. Maneuvering the reins with his left hand, while his right continued to hold the rifle's muzzle pointing unwaveringly at the center of Harrison's chest, he guided his horse to the left.

"What's your name, mister?" Harrison shouted after him.

Sitting sideways in the saddle, so that his rifle still covered the crowd, Gabe looked Harrison straight in the eye. "Conrad. Gabe Conrad."

"Fine," Harrison shouted back. "I'll have it chiseled on your tombstone."

The street took a sharp bend a few yards further on. Gabe kicked his horse into a slow trot, but as soon as he was around the bend, and out of sight of the crowd, he slowed the horse to a walk. The edge of town was only a couple of hundred yards away; the open country beyond beckoned. But instead of riding straight on out of town, as he might be expected to do, Gabe turned his horse into one of the narrow little alleyways that he'd earlier spotted from the hill. It was almost fully dark now. The alleyway swallowed horse and rider completely. As far as Gabe could tell, no one had seen him turn into the alley.

Hidden from view, but able to hear, and to see a little, too, Gabe waited. As he had expected, Harrison was not about to let him get away unmolested. "Johnny . . . Curly . . . take half a dozen o' the boys an' go after that son of a bitch. Bring me back his hide."

"Gawd, I dunno, boss," a voice came back. "You seen what he did to Pete an' his buddies. Killed all five of 'em."

"Goddamn it!" Harrison roared. "So . . . take *ten* men. He probably bushwhacked Pete an' the others, anyhow. But by Gawd, you better bring me back his ears. Hell, bring the whole carcass."

Within a few minutes, a dozen men had fetched their horses and were pounding wildly down the street that had supposedly been Gabe's escape route. Fine. The plan was working. The town had already been stripped of a dozen Slaughter cowhands, although Gabe had little doubt that at least that many remained. He'd seen the size of the herds that covered the country around the town. Herds that big needed a lot of punchers.

Gabe could have ridden away then, unmolested. But he knew that Harrison and his men had not yet learned the lesson that he had come here to teach them. So he rode farther down the alley. Using the mental map he'd drawn when he observed the town from above, he headed for the rear of the town's biggest saloon.

This particular saloon had a back door that opened out onto one of the alleys. Gabe tethered his horse in a little side alley, not too far from that back door. Then, still car-

rying his Winchester, he walked along the side wall of the
saloon, heading toward the main street. He stepped out onto
the boardwalk cautiously. No one seemed to have seen him
yet, for there was very little street lighting. He continued
on down the boardwalk and pushed his way in between the
saloon's swinging doors.

There were not many men inside; the action out in the
street had apparently emptied the place. Gabe saw only a
single cowhand, plus the two barflies who had been outside
in the crowd when he'd buffaloed Harrison and his men.
The two barflies had run right back to their spiritual home,
hoping to cadge a few free drinks by describing the excitement. So far, due to the lack of a crowd, they'd had lean
pickings. However, they recognized Gabe immediately; he
saw the recognition in their eyes, sensed their fear. Both
men stood frozen, half-clutching the bar with one hand,
their drinks with the other.

Gabe walked most of the length of the the the bar, finally
choosing a spot not far from the back door. Leaning his
rifle near his right leg, he hooked an arm over the bar, then
called out, "Bartender . . ."

The bartender couldn't have recognized him, because he
had not been out in the street when Gabe rode in. But the
two barflies had been talking up a storm about the mysterious
stranger, and about Harrison's reaction, so the bartender,
reading the fear in the eyes of those two worthies, had little
doubt who Gabe was.

Nevertheless, he walked over to his new customer, as
cool as could be. "What'll it be, stranger?" he asked.

"Sarsaparilla. Or root beer. Something that doesn't have
any alcohol in it," Gabe replied. Seeing the bartender's
disbelieving look, he added, "I don't drink spirits."

Which was true. Growing up among the Lakota, he had
seen what the white man's liquor could do to a man, the
havoc it could cause. He saw it now in the two ruined men
at the bar. Gabe knew, of course, that plenty of men were
able to drink and get away with it, but he was not sure he
fit that bill. He had no intention of finding out the hard way.

Shrugging, the bartender went to fetch his drink, and as

he did so, Gabe noticed the lone cowhand near the front of the bar slip furtively out through the swinging double doors, no doubt to spread the word, which fitted in just fine with Gabe's plan.

Gabe's drink turned out to be a root beer. Gabe loved root beer. He stood sipping slowly, but his eyes never left the saloon's swinging doors. His vigil was quickly rewarded. By the time he had drunk half his root beer, and was considering ordering another, the doors swung open, and three men came inside.

They looked like hard men, more gunmen than cowhands, although the state of their clothes indicated that punching cattle was the way they were currently earning their beans and bacon. Each of them wore a large-caliber revolver, and two of them had huge, man-sticker knives thrust into sheaths in their belts.

They spotted Gabe immediately and fanned out near the swinging doors. "Well, well, looky here," one of them drawled. "Here he is, hangin' out as sweet as pie, just like Jeff said."

The man who'd spoken was the deadliest-looking of the three, a tall, whipcord-thin man with eyes that said he liked killing people. His rig was the most practical, too; a big Colt worn low on his right hip, with enough leather cut away to give easy access to the pistol's butt, hammer, and trigger. Gabe quickly assessed the other two. The one on the first gunman's right looked just as dangerous, but the third man less so. He seemed to be a little scared.

"Harrison send you?" Gabe asked, slowly putting down his root beer.

"Uh-uh. But I figure he'll be along in a little while. Too late to do much, though, because we'll have already planted your bones, mister. I figure that'll be worth a nice little bonus."

"You're here to shoot, then," Gabe said softly. While his hands were now free, he nevertheless remained leaning against the bar, as if he did not have a worry in the world. But both his feet were planted firmly, and he was ready to move the moment he needed to. Three men. Bad odds.

If they acted together. But one of them, the nervous one, was showing signs of second thoughts. "Hey, Jack," he said to the one who'd just spoken. "Maybe we should wait for Harrison and the others. This gent—"

"Oh, shut the fuck up, Hank," Jack said disgustedly. "We're three to one. Just go for your piece and put a couple of slugs into the son of a bitch."

"Are you sure that three's enough?" Gabe asked softly. "So far, six of you have tried, and six of you have lost."

Jack showed his first trace of doubt. His eyes flicked from Gabe to his two companions, then back to Gabe. Now bravado replaced the doubt; he'd shot off his mouth in front of a number of people, and he had to make good his threats or eat crow.

But he needed to bolster his courage with a few more threats. Gabe was counting on that; as soon as he'd heard Jack's first words, he'd pegged him as the kind of cheap gunslinger who needed the help of his mouth to get him through tight spots. True to form, Jack couldn't resist one more verbal jab. "I can take you all by myself, you long-haired asshole. But I'm gonna give Hank an' Tom here a chance to have a little fun, too, 'cause we're gonna blow your . . ."

Gabe had long ago learned that few mouthy types were apt to make their move before they finished what they were saying—that's how important they considered the sound of their own voice. As Jack started his final sentence, Gabe was still standing casually, his right hand on the bar. The only guns his opponents could see were the rifle, effectively out of reach, and the pistol riding on his right hip, and with his right hand on the bar, the pistol did not seem to be much of a threat, either. Particularly considering the condition of Gabe's right hand. His right trigger finger, broken years ago in a fight, had not been set properly, but was twisted to one side at a sharp angle. More than one man had made the mistake of thinking that such a grotesquely bent finger would keep Gabe from shooting quickly and accurately.

Except that Gabe had no intention of using his right hand. He casually reached up toward his face with his left, as if

he were going to scratch his chin, but the hand never made
it to his face. Instead, he reached beneath his thunderbird
coat, his hand heading for the pistol hidden beneath his right
armpit.

There was nothing hurried about the movement, and
by the time Jack figured out what Gabe was doing, it was
too late. "Watch out, boys . . . he's goin' for it!" Jack
screamed, hunching his body as he reached for his own
pistol.

He was fast, Gabe had to give him that, but not fast
enough. The big .44–40 was already in Gabe's left hand,
with the right hand coming up off the bar to meet it. The
other two men were also going for their guns, and with
three opponents, Gabe could not enjoy the leisure of single,
well-aimed shots. He'd have to put out a lot of lead fast.

Gabe had a particular way of fanning a pistol. Instead of
simply slamming the edge of one hand down against the
hammer, which ruined a man's aim, he had learned to hold
the pistol with his right hand wrapped over his left hand,
and fan the hammer with his right thumb while his left
trigger finger held the trigger back. This two-handed grip
let him hold the .44 steady against the recoil, while at the
same time hosing bullets out of the muzzle as fast as his
thumb could work.

It all happened very quickly, but to Gabe, caught up in
the action, action that might see him dead in a few seconds,
it seemed quite slow and very deliberate. He got off two
shots before Jack got off his first. Jack's bullet went harm-
lessly into the floor, because Gabe's two bullets had already
slammed into the gunman's body, the first hitting him low
on the left side, the second in the throat.

Jack was still staggering backward when Gabe turned his
aim on the second man, who'd drawn only a moment later
than Jack. The man shot, but Gabe had been expecting it
and stepped to one side. It was a good shot; it hit the bar
where Gabe had been standing. The man cursed and pulled
back the hammer for another shot, but by now Gabe had
fired again. It was too hasty a shot, and the bullet only hit

the man in the leg, but it was a big bullet, and the man went down hard, howling.

Gabe swung his pistol toward the third man; he had only three shots left and couldn't afford to waste them. But the third man, Hank, stunned by the sudden outburst of gunfire, a thunderous roar that made the saloon's wooden walls shake, was scrambling as fast as he could toward the swinging doors. He'd dropped his pistol, and it was still in the air when he hit the doors. To encourage Hank to keep right on moving, Gabe snapped a shot after his retreating figure.

Only two rounds were left in the cylinder. Tom, the man Gabe had shot in the leg, was still down, gritting his teeth from the pain of the bullet in his leg. He'd dropped his pistol as he'd gone down, but was now reaching for it, glaring in Gabe's direction.

Gabe quickly walked forward. Standing over Tom, he thumbed the hammer back and aimed the barrel straight at Tom's head. "Don't even think about it," he snapped, his voice taut.

Tom looked up into the huge muzzle of the .44, swallowed a couple of times, then slowly moved his hand away from the fallen pistol. Gabe moved in closer and kicked the pistol several yards away. "Stay quiet and you'll stay alive," Gabe warned.

He moved over toward Jack. He was dead, eyes open and staring. Good. If he'd lived, he'd have probably ended up killing many a decent man.

Gabe heard a sound behind him. He spun, surveying the room. He saw only the two barflies. One had muttered something, but otherwise both of them remained frozen in place, their hands still wrapped around their drinks, their eyes huge with terror. The bartender had disappeared. "Nobody better come out from behind that bar with a scattergun," Gabe warned.

Nobody did. Gabe walked back to the bar, picked up his Winchester, and headed for the swinging doors. So far, since riding into town, he'd shot three men, killing one, wounding two, and he'd scared the hell out of a fourth. But there was still work to do.

Gabe walked along the boardwalk, totally alert, with all his senses heightened after half an hour of skating along the thin edge that separated living from dying. Naturally, the gunfire inside the saloon had been heard, and men were coming out into the street. Gabe passed a man who looked like a storekeeper. He took one look at Gabe, then ducked back into a doorway. A cowhand was not quite as sensible. Shouting out, "He's here! The bastard's still in town!" the cowhand made the mistake of reaching for his revolver.

Gabe shot him through the hip, an agonizing wound. The man screamed and fell. Gabe walked over to him. The cowhand looked up at him through eyes made huge by pain. "Don't shoot me no more, mister," he pleaded.

"I won't," Gabe replied, and walked on.

Two armed men came into sight. Gabe opened fire, levering rounds through the Winchester's chamber. One man clutched his arm, the other, after Gabe had put a bullet through the crown of his hat, beat a quick retreat.

Gabe continued on down the boardwalk, firing whenever he saw anything to fire at. He was not particularly intent on killing anyone, but would not have minded if he did. Within a couple of minutes he was driving several men ahead of him, firing steadily. Some fired back, but all were so shaken by his remorseless advance that they fired too wildly and missed.

Then Gabe saw Harrison stick his head out of a doorway about forty yards ahead. "Somebody git around behind him!" Harrison shouted. He appeared to be just about the only Slaughter cowhand still cool-headed enough to plan strategy.

Gabe's next two bullets gouged splinters from the doorway, and Harrison prudently ducked back out of sight. But he wasn't out of the fight. Gabe could hear him shouting orders from just inside the door.

Gabe fired a couple of more shots, the last his rifle contained, then he suddenly slipped smoothly to one side, disappearing into an alleyway. Nobody noticed at first, most of his opponents were keeping their heads down. Harrison was still trying to get the few men he had left to slip around behind Gabe, but one of them finally called out, "Hell, Don, we cain't see him!"

"Well . . . where the hell'd he go?" Harrison shouted back in a thoroughly disgruntled voice.

By now Gabe was walking silently down the alley, his feet treading carefully, and as he walked, he pushed new cartridges into the Winchester's loading gate. Men were running about aimlessly in the street. Gabe used his ears to keep track of them. Harrison's voice was still coming from the building in which he'd been hiding when Gabe disappeared.

Using his mental map of the town, Gabe located the rear of that building. There was one door. He tested the door latch. It was unlocked. Moving with incredible silence, he slipped inside the building. There was very little light, only a faint glimmer coming from an open inside doorway. Testing each floorboard, Gabe headed toward that door.

Finally reaching the doorway, he peered through it into another room, realizing that the faint gleam of light he'd noticed before was coming from the street, shining in through the open doorway that sheltered Harrison. Harrison was still there. At first Gabe could only hear his voice, shouting orders to the men outside. "Okay . . . you're far enough now. Come on back down the street. Flush the son of a bitch out into the open, then drive him on down to where I can shoot him."

"But we ain't *seen* him!" a plaintive voice called back.

"Goddamn it!" Harrison snarled. "He's gotta be out there somewhere!"

"Not necessarily," Gabe said softly.

He could see Harrison now; he saw him stiffen, then start to turn. "No!" Gabe snapped. "I'll blow your spine out!"

Harrison froze. Gabe walked forward quickly, took the revolver from Harrison's hand, then pulled him all the way back into the room and pushed him against a wall. Gabe moved close so that his face was only inches from Harrison's. There was very little light, but he could see the hatred in Harrison's eyes. Hatred and fear.

"I came here to deliver a message," Gabe said. "You

seem a little slow about understanding just what that message is.''

Harrison stared at him for a moment, then looked down at the rifle muzzle that was pointing up at his chin. ''Just what are you trying to say?'' he finally asked.

''What I said before. If any of your men molest Los Robles, or any other peaceful village, I'll hunt them down and kill them . . . after I've killed you. Is that simple enough?''

Gabe raised the muzzle of his rifle a little higher, forcing Harrison's chin upward. Harrison nodded in quick little jerks. ''Good,'' Gabe murmured. ''I'm glad we could agree on something. Now . . . *adios, hombre.*''

Gabe turned and walked from the room, heading through the building toward the back door that led into the alley. For a few seconds all was quiet from Harrison's room, then Gabe heard a quick pounding of bootheels, and he knew that Harrison had run outside into the street. ''Here . . . he's in here!'' Harrison screamed to his men.

Naturally, they came running, but by then Gabe was halfway down the alley. ''No . . . no . . . in back,'' he heard Harrison shout. Gabe had already reached his horse. He mounted, then guided the animal out the back side of town, heading toward the trail that led up into the surrounding hills.

He had ridden only a few hundred yards when he heard the thunder of hooves coming from farther up the trail. He immediately pulled his horse into some thick brush. A moment later a dozen horsemen came thundering by, riding hell for leather toward the town. It was the men whom Harrison had sent out earlier. Hearing all the gunfire coming from the town, they were racing back to help their friends— way too late.

After they'd passed, Gabe rode back onto the trail again. A few minutes later he was back on the hilltop from which he'd earlier observed the town. Below him, men were milling around in the main street. Torches had been lit. Gabe saw men cautiously working their way into the dark mouths of alleys. He spotted Harrison holding a torch. Harrison turned then and faced toward the darkness beyond the town. Apparently he was beginning to realize that the man he was after had flown the coop. Gabe heard his angry, frustrated shout, heard his voice float up from below. ''You'll hang, you bastard! I'll see that you swing, if it's the last thing I ever do!''

''It just might be,'' Gabe said softly. Then he turned his horse and rode away into the mountains.

CHAPTER EIGHT

Gabe rode straight up into the Sangre de Cristos. Harrison may have organized a pursuit, but Gabe saw none of it. He had effectively disappeared into a strange and beautiful world far different from the plains and valleys that lay below.

Here there were trees, canyons, fast, cold little streams, but above all, trees. Gabe had been born and raised on the northern plains, where trees were rare, so the sudden abundance of spruce, pine, poplar, and cottonwood fascinated him. Particularly the cottonwoods. That first morning in the mountains, he stopped at the first cottonwood grove he came across, dismounted, and sat beneath the trees, listening to the wind shake the broad spear-point leaves all around and above him.

Mounting again, he rode farther into the mountains, careful to use every trick he knew to hide his trail. Eventually he found a small, isolated valley, with a quiet little stream running down its center. It felt right. He decided that this would be a good place to stay for a while.

First he would need supplies. After making camp and staking out his horse, he slipped away up the canyon with his Sharps. When he was well away from the camp, he sat down beside the stream to wait. Now he began to let go of white man's time and return to Indian time, which was "no time." There was only now, this living moment. Since all that was happening around him was equal, Gabe spent a timeless half hour looking down into the streambed, noticing

how the water's tiny ripples refracted the light, casting small
bands of light onto the underwater rocks, giving them the
appearance of a tortoise's mottled shell. Cottonwood leaves
floated lazily by, bobbing gently on tiny wavelets, in no
more of a hurry than Gabe.

Finally, there was movement from farther up the canyon,
something big. Gabe looked up, saw a large buck mule deer
step out of a small grove of aspens. Gabe remained motionless for another few seconds, watching the deer, lost in
the beauty of its movements. How daintily it moved for
such a large animal. He watched the buck turn its head,
sniff the air, scout the nearby bushes for wolf or mountain
lion, while all the time, unknowing, it was in easy range
of the most deadly enemy of all.

Gabe slowly raised the Sharps. He murmured a quiet
apology to the deer, then pressed the trigger. Perhaps the
deer heard him, for it looked up just as the rifle roared. It
was too late. The deer leaped high into the air as the bullet
struck, one last mighty leap. Then it fell to the ground,
where it lay motionless, dead upon a bed of aspen leaves.

Gabe immediately reloaded the Sharps; he never left a
gun empty. Then he walked to the deer. It was dead; the
large dark eyes had already lost their shine. Gabe apologized
to the deer one last time for taking its life. He thanked it
for its meat.

It was a big deer, too big to easily carry, so Gabe decided
to butcher it on the spot. Hanging it from a tree limb by its
rear legs, he cut its throat to let the blood run out. Then he
cut open the deer's thorax and gutted it. He worked quickly
and expertly, and as he worked, he smiled ruefully. How
low the mighty hunter had fallen. In the old days, this would
have been woman's work.

Although he worked quickly, he was particularly careful
about skinning the deer, for he would have a special use
for its hide. Finally, he quartered the carcass, then carried
the meat and the hide back to his camp. It took several
trips. No hurry, no hurry. This was . . . life. To be lived,
not rushed. Rushing only brought closer the inevitability of
one's death. Which would come soon enough.

Working efficiently but leisurely, Gabe cut saplings and made a drying rack at the edge of his campsite. Then he sliced most of the meat into thin strips and hung the strips on the rack. Gathering wood, he built a fire beneath the rack. He would keep the fire going for a long time, and its slow heat and smoke would dry the meat. After most of the moisture had been cooked from the flesh, it would keep for a long time.

However, he saved an entire haunch to cook whole and eat fresh. Fastening the meat onto a spit, he roasted it over a hot fire, searing the outside of the meat quickly. When the venison was partially cooked, he cut chunks off the outside, from the more cooked portion, and ate it. It was delicious. He savored the rich juices and meaty taste. Later, he would cook the haunch a little more, searing the outside portion again, assuring a continuing supply of fresh-cooked meat.

No hurry, no hurry. His belly full, Gabe carefully scraped the fat off the inside of the deer hide. He did not intend to completely tan the hide, but now it wouldn't smell as much, and it would have some suppleness.

By the time he had finished with the hide, the day was nearly over. Using sticks, Gabe dug out a shallow pit near the stream, more than six feet long and three feet wide. Then he walked over to a small stand of pine trees and began collecting pine needles, which he brought back and used to fill up the pit. He spread his bedroll on top of the pine needles. Now he had a bed.

He slid into the bedroll. Wonderful. His new bed was soft, but did not sag, and it had the fresh, clean smell of pine trees. He lay on his back as the darkness came, watching the world fade away from around him, until he could only hear it, hear the gentle chuckle of the stream, hear the night breeze drifting aimlessly through the cottonwood trees. He went to sleep looking up at a skyful of stars through a black network of tree branches. He woke when the morning sun was just touching the tops of the tallest trees.

He got up, stretched, and went over to check his horse, making certain that the animal had access to feed. Then he took off his white man's clothing and hung it on tree limbs to air out, along with his bedding. Next he went down to the stream and washed. There had been too much riding, too much fighting, killing. It was time to clean it all away.

But washing in the stream would not be enough. He needed washing inside as well as outside—he must scour his spirit. He needed *inipi*.

Naked, he roamed the area, looking for stones—not just any stones, but stones of the right kind. Within ten minutes he had found a dozen, each about four or five inches thick, stones that would neither explode nor crumble when they grew hot.

Next he began to gather wood, dry wood that would not smoke, but would give off great heat. After he'd gathered enough, he laid down four good-sized pieces, stacking them so that they pointed north-south, then stacked four more on top of the first four, pointing east-west. The stones he had collected went on top of the wood. Using kindling, he set fire to the wood. He waited until the fire was burning well, heating the stones stacked on top. Then he went down to the stream and cut seven willow saplings, which he brought back to the fire.

The stones were doing well, and he could feel growing heat radiating from them. Now it was time to build the lodge. After carefully choosing a spot not too far from the fire, a spot with the right kind of feeling, he used his knife to dig seven small holes, forming a circle about seven feet across. Next he peeled the bark from the saplings, then stuck the bigger end of each sapling into one of the holes, tamping down the earth until they were firmly held in place. He then dug a shallow pit in the center of the circle.

Next, he bent the saplings inward, using strips of bark to tie them in place, until he had formed the skeleton of a small dome about four feet high. Satisfied, he scouted the area, collecting several clumps of sage. He spread some of the sage on the ground inside the dome, at the north side, where it would form a comfortable place to sit. Other bundles of sage were stacked loosely near the first bundle, where they would be easy to reach.

He went over to check the deerskin. It was not very pliable, but it would do. He draped it over the sapling dome as a cover, then added his blankets. Not enough. He added his clothing and his thunderbird coat and finally the dome was covered. He now had a complete sweat lodge, relatively airtight. It was time for *inipi*.

Gabe checked the stones. They were ready, glowing almost white from the heat. Using a pair of forked sticks that he had cut, he carried the stones one by one into the sweat lodge and placed them in the central pit, then laid burning coals on top of the stones.

Going to where he had stacked his gear, he picked up his canteen and the deerskin pouch that contained his pipe, then crawled inside the sweat lodge, pulling a flap of deer hide across the opening after him.

It was dark inside, but not completely dark. There was light from the glowing coals and from daylight filtering in through tiny chinks in the outside covering. While his eyes adjusted to the gloom, Gabe took his pipe from its pouch. Gabe had owned this particular pipe for years. It was quite a long pipe, almost as long as his arm. The stem was made of hollowed out willow, the bowl of a soft red stone that was found only in Minnesota. Four strips of colored cloth and an eagle feather hung from the stem. The strips of cloth represented the four directions, and the eagle feather represented *Wakan Tanka*, the Great Spirit, the highest entity of which a man could conceive.

Gabe held the pipe close to his body, sliding his fingers along the wooden shaft, worn smooth by years of handling, then caressed the soapy-feeling pipestone that made up its bowl. This was no ordinary pipe, no simple instrument for enjoying the pleasures of tobacco. This was a ceremonial pipe, one with a special history. It had been given to Gabe by an old Oglala warrior and medicine man, Two Face, just minutes before the Army hanged him. This pipe had power, the power of Two Face's life and death. This pipe, and the smoking of it, was one of the ways a man could approach the mystery of *Wakan Tanka*, the mystery of all that was beyond normal human understanding.

Gabe filled the pipe's bowl with *chanshasha*, a mixture of wild tobacco and willow bark. Then, holding the pipe's bowl in his left hand, the stem in his right, he solemnly presented the pipe to the four directions—west, north, east, and south—then held it low, close to the earth, and high, toward the sky.

This ritual completed, Gabe took a coal from the fire and placed it inside the pipe bowl, lighting the tobacco. Raising the pipe to his lips, he drew in a lungful of smoke, pungent smoke that seared his throat, but as the smoke went into him, he felt power entering with it; strength, peace, and a mystic connection with *Wakan Tanka*.

When he felt he had smoked enough, he knocked the remaining tobacco onto the coals. It burned quickly, filling the sweat lodge with its rich odor. Gabe threw some of the sage on top of the coals. It burst into flame, and he inhaled the acrid smell of burning sage.

By now, it was very hot inside the sweat lodge. Gabe could feel heat pricking at his skin. He watched the red glow of the coals slowly die away. When the last of their light had gone, it was possible to see the hot, reddish glow of the stones. Gabe picked up his canteen. He poured a little of the water over his head, then, using a handmade dipper, he poured water over the glowing stones.

The water hissed and crackled against the stones. Steam quickly filled the sweat lodge, and now Gabe was sweating copiously, his skin burning from the intense heat. He poured more water onto the stones. There was a sharp report, like a rifle shot. One of the stones had split into two pieces. More steam hissed into the stifling air.

Sweat poured from Gabe's body, ran down his face, stung his eyes. He could hardly breathe. The steam began to diminish again, so Gabe poured water on the stones for the third time. More steam arose, closing around his body like a fiery blanket. Hot, purifying steam.

A little later he poured water on the stones for the fourth and final time. Already a feeling of peace, of wholeness, was settling over his body, soaking into his inner being. The dross and dirt, both mental and physical, that he had been aware of for too long was being washed away. He was becoming whole again, one being, one with that which . . . that which could not be expressed in words. His *ni*, that energy which a man takes into himself the way he takes in air, was cleansed, was strong and pure again.

As the last of the steam died away, Gabe took his canteen and the pipe and crawled out into the open, into the clean, fresh mountain air. Naked, he ran to the stream and threw himself into its coolness. He lay in the water, unmoving, letting it flow over him, letting it wash away the sweat and smoke.

When the water began to feel too cold, he left the stream and lay in the sun. After a while he got up and went over to his saddlebags. He pulled out a wide strip of cloth, from which he fashioned a simple breechclout so that he would not be completely naked, but so that the sun and wind would be able to reach most of his body. Free of his white man's raiment, but suspecting he would need it again, Gabe spent the next hour washing his clothing and bedding, then hung everything out to dry on the bushes that surrounded his camp. Then he lay on his back on his bed, looking up into the trees, watching birds bicker among the branches. Ah, how peaceful it was, the aloneness of this moment.

He knew that eventually the aloneness would become a burden. He was a man, and men needed the company of other men. A few were able to live solitary lives. Gabe had met men who did; mostly white men, trappers, living alone in the most remote parts of the Rocky Mountains. But they were white, they had been born so much more alone than the red man, who, despite his small numbers, or perhaps because of it, lived a rich tribal life, secure in the closeness of family and tribe, seldom completely alone.

It was a way of life now gone, along with the buffalo and the open range. Gabe had never found, among the myriad complexities of the white man's way, anything that satisfied him the way the old life had satisfied him. Nothing that answered a man's questions about the world in such a beautiful way, a way of unity with the mystery that surrounded life itself. The white man had nothing as cleansing or as unifying as *inipi*. The confessions the white man's priests wrung from the believer fostered not freedom, but guilt and dependency. Gabe had found nothing as warm and secure as the life he had known with his tribe. Nothing that connected him to the earth in as satisfying away as the idea of *Wakan Tanka* did.

But there was one thing he had learned from the white man . . . a new concept of time. Time moving, but only in one direction, toward the future. Always toward the future. There was no going back. That which had once been was now lost forever.

CHAPTER NINE

Gabe remained at his camp for three more days, mending gear, cleaning guns, patching his clothes, but mostly just resting or idly wandering, half-naked, clad only in breech-clout and moccasins, quietly enjoying the beauty of his little valley.

Eventually he began to grow restless. On the fourth day he saddled his horse, which had been growing restless, too. Gabe debated putting his white man's clothing back on, but decided he would not need to. So, wearing his breechclout and moccasins, with a pistol strapped around his waist and a rifle in one hand, he rode bareback out of the valley, his long hair blowing free in the wind, his big slouch hat left behind.

For a while he rode aimlessly, exercising himself and his mount. It was half an hour before he realized that he was riding in the general direction of the town in which he'd shot up Harrison's men. He almost turned his horse around, but he finally decided that maybe he was here for a reason. He'd left a maddened beehive behind in that town. It made him uncomfortable to not know what was happening there.

He did not have to ride all the way to the town to find out. He was about two miles away, still well up in the mountains when he caught sight of movement well below him, about half a mile distant. Horsemen.

He immediately guided his horse into a stand of pines. Since he was quite a bit higher than the riders, there was not much chance of them spotting him . . . if he was careful.

Dismounting, he worked his way to the edge of the pine trees and looked down.

There were about twenty of them, riding bunched up. They seemed to be heavily armed; he could see the glitter of sunlight shining off weapons. They were riding slowly, as if looking for a sign. Gabe immediately regretted that he had not brought his binoculars. Sometimes the white man's way had its advantages.

He watched the men below for half an hour. Were they Harrison's men, out looking for him? Possibly. Hell, probably.

Gabe watched until he was certain the riders below were not heading in the direction of his camp. Then he mounted and rode back to the valley. But the valley was no longer the same there. The peace of the mountains had been shattered.

The next day he rode out again, but this time with all his gear strapped to his horse, in case he decided to ride completely out of the area. He headed for the same place where he'd seen the riders the day before. Sure enough, at about the same time of morning, he saw what appeared to be the same group heading up into the mountains. This time he had his binoculars. Crawling on his belly to the edge of a cliff, he carefully studied the men below. They leaped into focus; hard-looking men, cowhands, gunmen, riding with what looked like grim intent.

This time, when the men headed up into the mountains, they took a slightly different route. It occurred to Gabe that they must be making a systematic search. For him? Once again, probably. Apparently, Harrison didn't accept defeat easily.

Anger surged through Gabe. He had originally ridden to that damned town to deliver a message, to warn Harrison and any other Slaughter men to leave the local people alone. Apparently Harrison had not yet digested that message. Gabe contemplated slipping into town during the night so that he could reinforce Harrison's memory. Maybe even permanently solve the problem . . . as far as Harrison was concerned.

Better yet, why not just ride completely out of the area, head up toward Colorado, where there were more mountains—higher mountains—and more isolation. He could leave all this trouble behind him. After all, wasn't he a free man, a wanderer, a man with no attachments?

He rode back to his camp in a troubled state of mind. He did not like being pressured. His pride told him to stay and fight. His common sense said to ride on out. He compromised by deciding to stay for another day.

During the night he made up his mind to ride on. It was only a matter of time until the hunters found his camp. By noon the next day he was packing his gear. He was trying to figure out how much of the dried venison his horse could carry when he became aware of movement near the lower mouth of the valley. At first he thought it was a deer, then he saw a horse. A horse with a rider.

Gabe immediately reached for his Sharps. Was it a lone rider just happening by, as he himself had happened by? Then he saw two more horsemen behind the first.

Gabe glanced toward the upper end of the valley, looking for more horsemen. He had to know if they'd boxed him in, if he'd be running into an ambush if he tried to ride out that way. He'd have to make up his mind quickly; there were more and more horsemen riding into the valley's lower end. Damn! They'd found him more quickly than he'd expected!

Gabe leaped up onto his horse's back. The hell with the rest of the meat, he was going to have enough trouble saving his own hide. He was pulling his horse's head around, ready to race away up the valley—damn the possibility of ambushes from that direction—when one of the men below sang out, "*Hola* . . . Señor Conrad!"

The man was speaking Spanish. Gabe twisted in the saddle, staring hard at the rider who'd called out. It was Don Javier! Gabe reined in his horse. The animal, having already picked up its master's agitation, pranced nervously.

More and more men were riding into the valley. Gabe estimated their number at thirty or forty. They continued up the valley, riding straight toward him, with Don Javier in the lead. He let them come, but he also kept his Sharps ready, his thumb on the hammer, ready to pull it back into full cock.

He was reassured by the smile on Don Javier's face. The old man rode straight up to him. "You are a hard man to find, Señor Conrad. We would not have known where to look if one of our people had not spotted your campsite a day ago while he was out hunting. Let us hope that the others have not had similar good luck."

"The others?"

The smile faded from Don Javier's face. "Yes. The Slaughter men. They ride out to look for you every day."

Gabe nodded. "I saw them."

"They might get lucky."

Gabe waved a hand toward the north. "Not if I'm not here for them to find."

Don Javier shook his head sadly. "There is more to this than Slaughter and his men. There is the law to consider."

"The law?"

"Yes. You've been charged with murder, with the killing of all those Slaughter men. There's a warrant for your arrest. Those are not just bands of vengeful cowboys out looking for you, those are legal posses, led by lawmen. Wherever you go, this charge of murder will follow. You are a hunted man, Señor Conrad, and someday, someone will catch up to you."

Gabe did not quite know what to say. He remembered how the Army had hanged Two Face the day he'd given Gabe his pipe for a crime the old man had not even committed. Two Face had been returning a white woman who'd been captured by another tribe. He'd decided to do this as a gesture of friendship toward the whites. They had hanged him for it. Of course, Two Face had, en route, forced the woman to sleep with him. What else were women for? For this they had hanged him. Just the other day Gabe had killed many men. They would hang him even higher than they'd hanged Two Face.

He looked at the men surrounding him. They were all

heavily armed, all looking grim. "Are you here to fight for me?" he asked Don Javier.

The old man shook his head. "No. Eventually, they would overwhelm us."

Once again Gabe studied the men, their weapons, their faces. "Then why are you here?"

"To take you in."

Gabe's hand closed more tightly around the stock of his Sharps. Don Javier saw the move, and eased the tension by laughing. "We want to take you in under our protection. We think that you should stand trial and get this trouble behind you."

"Stand trial?"

"Yes."

Don Javier turned in his saddle to face a much younger man. "Ramon. Help me, please."

The younger man rode up beside Don Javier. "This is Ramon Garcia," Don Javier told Gabe. "Ramon is a lawyer. We sent him back east to law school. He has just returned. Now, perhaps the law will be for us, too."

Gabe studied Ramon dubiously. He was a good-looking man, in his middle to late twenties. His expression was very earnest. So were his words. "We can take you to a town that is friendly to us," Ramon said. "The judge is one of the few honest ones. The jury will be chosen locally. They'll be sympathetic."

"And I'm to risk my neck on that?" Gabe asked.

"We'll protect your neck with our own necks," Ramon replied, even more earnestly. "We, all of us, owe you a great deal. After all, it was on our behalf that you got yourself in this trouble. We have our honor to consider, Señor Conrad."

Gabe sat his horse for a full minute, thinking. No one disturbed him. Instinct warned him to ride away, to disappear into the wilderness, where no one would find him. The trouble with that plan was that true wilderness was getting harder and harder to find. Civilization was pushing in everywhere. There was a strong possibility that he would be systematically hunted down. He did not want that; it was not his custom to run from a fight. "We'll do it your way," he said curtly.

Don Javier's and Ramon's answering smiles were grim ones. "We may not succeed," Don Javier said. "And then there will be a fight. We will not let them hang you while any of us remain alive."

Gabe nodded. There wasn't much he could say.

It took only a few minutes to apportion the rest of the dried meat among Don Javier's men. But before he left the valley, Gabe pulled down the frame of his sweat lodge and scattered it among the trees. Don Javier and the others watched him curiously, but none intruded, none queried him. Finally they rode away. Gabe looked back over his shoulder at the valley. This had been a good place, but like most good places, there was always a time for leaving.

Gabe counted the men with Don Javier. Forty-two. Together, they rode down out of the mountains into the plain, heading toward a town somewhat larger than Don Javier's town. This was the county seat for the area. They were still several miles away when they spotted a body of men riding in their direction. Don Javier swore quietly. "I had hoped we would reach town without them finding us," he said, obviously a little worried.

The strangers galloped right up to them. There were about twenty, all well armed. "Hey!" one of them shouted, his Texas twang obvious. "There's our man!"

They fanned out around Don Javier's men, who bunched up around Gabe. He wished they would spread out more. That would be better if it came to a fight. The two groups eyed one another warily. Finally a man rode out from among the newcomers. "Name's Hanks," he said curtly to Don Javier, correctly choosing him as the group's leader. "Deputy outta Bernalillo County. Got a warrant for Gabe Conrad. That man there. Gonna take him in."

Don Javier shook his head. "You're a little late, deputy."

"What the hell do you mean, late?" Hanks demanded, bristling.

Don Javier turned toward one of his riders, a slender, moustached man. "Jesus. Inform the man."

Jesus rode forward to confront Hanks. "I, too, am a deputy, Señor Hanks. And I have already arrested this man. We are taking him to jail to stand trial."

"That ain't necessary," Hanks snapped. "I'll take him off your hands."

"*Señor*," Jesus said quietly. "I do not give up my prisoners. I have arrested him . . . he will go to my jail."

"The hell, you say!" Hanks blustered. "We're gonna hang this bastard down in Albuquerque. Now, hand him over."

"Over my dead body, *señor*," Jesus said just as quietly, but there was no mistaking the steel in his voice. Gabe began to realize that Jesus was a very hard-looking man. Hanks began to realize it, too. He had been mentally counting the men with Jesus, and the count was not comforting. "Hell!" he blustered. "The son of a bitch ain't even had his fuckin' guns took away! Harrison ain't gonna like this. Slaughter, neither."

Jesus smiled. It was a cold smile. "I am desolated for them, Señor Hanks. Now . . . get your men out of our way. We are taking the prisoner in."

Hanks appeared about to speak again; Gabe could see his throat muscles working. Finally, Hanks contented himself with a muttered curse, then pulled his horse out of the way. The men behind him did the same. There were a few moments of tension as Don Javier's group rode close to the Texans, but then they were past, riding closed up around Gabe.

As they rode on, Gabe felt increasingly uneasy. He did not like this feeling of having his fate in the hands of others. His unease only increased once they had reached the town. It would be easy to get trapped here.

Jesus took him directly to the town's small jail, which also served as the sheriff's office. Gabe was relieved to see that the sheriff was of Spanish descent. He welcomed Don Javier and the others amiably, especially his deputy. "So, Jesus," he said with mock gravity, "once again you've brought your man back alive."

Jesus smiled. "And I intend to keep him alive."

Which might not be that easy. Naturally, Hanks had spread the word, and within two hours cattlemen began riding into town, all of them heavily armed. But many from the Spanish-speaking population began riding in, too, until Don Javier's party amounted to over a hundred men.

Gabe remained housed in the jail, the most defensible building in town. Its thick adobe walls and barred windows would not be easy to rush. For appearance sake, Gabe was now without his weapons, although they lay on a tabletop where they would be accessible if he needed them. Gabe finally retired to one of the cells to sleep. The cell door was not locked.

After an hour's nap, Gabe got up from his cot and looked out the window. Groups of cowboys had formed. A man spotted him. "There's that son of a bitch now!" the man cried out. "Looking back at us, bold as brass."

"Hang him!" someone else shouted. An ugly murmur ran through the crowd. They drifted a little closer to the jail. Gabe watched them, wondering for the hundredth time if he'd done the right thing, entrusting his life to the white man's law.

Jesus, having heard the shouting, came into the cell and looked out the window. He studied the crowd for a moment. By now there were about fifty men grouped together, most of them glaring at Gabe's cell window. Jesus went back into the jail. Gabe heard quiet orders being given, and within a couple of minutes, men with rifles were posted in the cells on either side of his cell. They thrust their rifles through the cell windows, ostentatiously covering the crowd.

Night fell. Now Gabe could not see outside. But he could hear. Hear the shouting of drunken cowhands, hear the cries for his blood. But with a hundred armed men surrounding the jail, there were no overt moves to lynch him.

Ramon came in to see him an hour before midnight. "We just got a telegram," he said. "The judge will be here tomorrow morning."

"If they let him."

Ramon shrugged. "Even the gringos are careful about molesting judges. If they did, no matter what the reason, the full weight of the government would come down on them. The judge will arrive.''

"What kind of man is he?''

"A fair man. One who believes in the rule of law, rather than than the rule of men.''

Ramon stayed a little while longer, discussing the next day's trial. After he had left, Gabe, knowing there was not much he could do, lay down to sleep. All during his life, death had been an ever-present possibility, his constant companion. There were worse things than death. He considered useless worry much worse, a self-destructive way of living, dominated by the many little deaths a man suffered by agonizing over that which could not be helped. Death was, after all, inevitable . . . although the thought of being hanged filled him with repugnance. Before falling asleep, he decided, irrevocably, that if Ramon's plan were to fail, if he were sentenced to hang, he would try to escape, no matter what the odds. He would force the bastards to kill him in a fair fight.

Morning came, along with the news that the judge had arrived during the night. At eight o'clock Gabe was marched out of the jail to the courthouse. A ring of armed men surrounded him, with those men in turn surrounded by a large crowd. But today the crowd was different; all during the night people had been coming into town. Gabe heard many cries of support as he was led into the courtroom.

There was not enough room inside to hold everyone who wanted to watch the show; the crowd spilled outside into the street. Gabe sat down at a table next to Ramon. He saw Don Javier sitting in one of the front benches reserved for spectators. With a start, he saw Elena sitting not far from Don Javier. She looked straight at him, gave him a quick, somewhat strained smile. Suddenly he felt better. He smiled back.

Gabe's attention was diverted by the pounding of a gavel. He looked up at the bench. The judge was a severe-looking man in his late forties. He sat behind his high desk, impassive, not paying much attention to anyone. The gavel rapped again. Finally the court was called to order. The court clerk read out the charge against Gabe. The trial had begun.

The actual trial was rather anti-climactic. A jury was impaneled, and since juries must be chosen from local voters, and almost all the local voters were of Spanish descent, the jury was decidedly Latin, with only one Anglo on it, but he owned a local store and he knew which side of his bread held the butter.

Witnesses were called. Slaughter's men described the action at Harrison's headquarters. Several people from Don Javier's village described the terrorizing of their town by Slaughter's men, the shooting of the old man, the murder of the boy, the way Elena had been molested.

Elena was called to the stand. She testified calmly, demure and beautiful. When she described how her blouse had been ripped half off her body by the drunken cowhand, a growl arose from the jury, a growl both of outrage and of fascination as each juror tried to imagine just how a half-naked Elena might look.

It was all over in less than two hours. The jurors did not even leave the room, but conferred for a moment in whispers, with much nodding among them. Then the foreman stood up and gave the verdict. "Not guilty by reason of self-defense."

The judge, who had done very little to interrupt the proceedings other than to calm down overexcited witnesses, rapped his gavel. Gabe was a free man.

But not necessarily a man destined to live a long life. As he walked out of the courthouse, he was aware of ugly glares from many cowhands, although quite a few seemed, after the trial, to bear him no ill will. "Well, like the jury told us," one of them said within Gabe's hearing, "it was self-defense, plain as the nose on your face."

Gabe glanced in the direction of the voice. He saw a lanky cowhand standing with several others. The cowhand's eyes met Gabe's, then the cowhand turned back to his companions. "By golly," he said, shaking his head ruefully. "That musta been some fight, that there hombre 'gainst five hard men. An' he took down ever' one of 'em. Sure would o' liked to o' saw it.''

Not all of his companions were as fond of fair play. Gabe ran the gauntlet of their glares all the way back to the jail. He felt relieved when he had retrieved his weapons. ''Well. . . now what?'' Ramon asked Gabe, who was standing, armed, near the jailhouse door.

''I'm not sure.''

''We're going to ride out of town with you for a while,'' Jesus cut in. ''Out there you'll run across men with hard feelings.''

''I know.''

Gabe felt a hand on his arm. It was Don Javier. He looked into the old man's eyes, aware that they were not the eyes of an ordinary old man—this was a man among men. ''Come and stay with us in our town, the town you helped save,'' Don Javier said. ''You would be doing us an honor.''

Gabe stared at Don Javier, only partly comprehending. Stay? In a town? For a man like himself, was that ever a real possibility? He remembered then the sense of belonging he had once felt, living among the People. But still he hesitated.

Don Javier spoke again. ''There is someone in particular who would be especially happy if you would come and live among us.''

''Who?'' Gabe asked woodenly, although he already knew. Looking out the door, he saw her coming across the town plaza toward the jail. Elena. And as he saw her, saw the beauty of her, especially saw the way she was looking at him, he knew that he would accept.

CHAPTER TEN

"¡Al derecho!" Pedro shouted. Gabe could barely hear Pedro's voice over the surrounding noise, but he understood, so he kicked his horse to the right, where a steer was trying to break free of the herd. Cutting toward the steer's off side, Gabe choused the frightened animal back in with the rest of the cattle.

He was with half a dozen Los Robles men, several miles from town, rounding up the small herd of cattle that the men of the village owned communally. Damn, but it was hot and dusty! Gabe raised the tail of his long bandanna and wiped his face, which did little more than redistribute the grime. He made a sour face. He'd never imagined he'd end up being a cowboy.

Or *vaquero*, as the local people called it. *Vaquero*. A literal translation being, "one who works with cows." Ramon, who had seen much more of the United States than any other person in Los Robles except Gabe, had spent many hours telling Gabe of his impressions of that big world "out there." It was not that Ramon was vain about his knowledge, it was simply that he enjoyed the knowledge for its own sake, and enjoyed going over it again and again, as a man who loves wine will taste the same vintage many times.

One afternoon Ramon and Gabe were riding stirrup to stirrup, returning from a trip to the county seat, where Ramon had filed some legal papers on behalf of the village. Ramon liked to talk as he rode. "It was the Spanish *vaquero*

who taught the gringo cowboys most of what they know,"
he explained to Gabe. "When the gringos first came to
Texas, sixty or so years ago, they found us Latinos riding
herd on vast numbers of cattle. At that time there were far
more cattle in Texas than there were people. By then, the
vaquero himself was a blend of Spanish and Indian, although
you must never say that to a Latino . . . he'll cut your heart
out, even if he's ninety-percent Indian. We all pride ourselves on being pure Spanish . . . descended from nobility,
of course."

Ramon's grin was designed to let Gabe know that this
was their little joke to share. He continued. "The *vaqueros*
practically lived on the backs of their horses, they were a
part of them. And when the gringos came—before they
stole the land—they copied the way the Latinos worked
their cattle, even copied the names of their gear: lariat for
latigo; chaps for *chaparrajos*; cayuse for *caballo*; hoosgow
for *huzgado*, and many, many other names. They also used
our Spanish stock saddles and our bits and our branding
irons. But, *señor*, they never learned to ride like us."

So saying, Ramon laughed and rode off at a mad gallop,
sitting his horse with nonchalant ease.

Gabe had to admit, these people could ride. They were
practically born on the back of a horse. In that way they
reminded him of his own people, the Oglala, who also rode
as if they were part of their mount. There were other ways
the local Spanish resembled the Oglala, such as their ten-
dency to let tomorrow take care of itself. Gabe liked that.

However, there were many ways in which the Spanish
and the Oglala were agonizingly different, agonizing to
Gabe, who was doing his best to adapt to the local way of
life. Partly, it was the settled existence the New Mexico
Spanish lived and their rather rigid code of conduct that
gave him the most trouble. The Oglala, like other Lakota,
had moved their villages often, either to follow the buffalo
or to find a good place to winter, or simply for the pleasure
of moving to a new place. The people of Los Robles stuck
to their town as if their souls were rooted into its dry soil.

There were bright spots. Like the Oglala, the local Spanish left the real drudgery in the hands of the women. The men herded cattle, gambled, staged cockfights, and drank, while the women cooked and cleaned and scrubbed and gathered. Also, the men of Los Robles were just as jealous of their honor as the Oglala. They were very quick to take offense at the smallest imagined slight.

Unfortunately, a good deal of a Latino's honor revolved around his womenfolk, around the rather metaphysical question of whether they were "pure" or not. It was an absolute obsession, this worrying over the condition of a woman's body—to be exact, her sexual parts. True, Gabe's Oglala had encouraged their women to be virtuous, but there had been a good deal of leeway. Young men and women spent a lot of time together, could make love under certain conditions. Not among the Latinos. To do so was to invite a blood feud with the girl's relatives. What most confused Gabe was, on the one hand, the level of sensuality, of half-hidden sexuality that throbbed in the veins of the people of Los Robles, and on the other hand, the stern repression of this sexuality. No wonder tempers boiled over so easily, no wonder the young men leaped so eagerly into games of daring and danger, into the gushing blood of the cockfight, or the slow killing of bulls.

Gabe might not have been so intensely aware of this dichotomy if it had not been for Elena. She was beautiful, she exuded sensuality—a great deal of it pointed in Gabe's direction—and worst of all was the undeniable fact of her simply being here, close, apparently available . . . but at the same time as remote as the moon. Gabe, confused by the local mating customs, which were so different from both those of the whites and of the Lakota, did not quite know what to do. And it was driving him crazy. Gabe was not a man to savor pleasure deferred.

That particular afternoon, riding back from the roundup, Gabe was half in a mood to pack his gear and ride away, to ride out once again into the vastness of the land, ride away from these narrow streets and dark buildings. To sleep under the stars again and, as he went to sleep, not have any idea which direction he might choose for the next day's ride.

What had kept him here so far was the people, their obvious liking for him, their general cheerfulness, their innate warmth, their love of life. And Elena, of course. The thought of her was always his strongest tie to Los Robles ... to look into her large, dark eyes, to see the way the soft swell of her breasts rose and fell a little more quickly beneath her white blouse when she drew near him, to see the way those eyes looked at him, to be aware of the intoxicating female odor of her, to suspect that she wanted him as much as he wanted her ...

Was she waiting for him to approach her old grandfather—both her parents were dead, and her brother had been killed the day Gabe rode into town—and ask for her hand in marriage? He smiled as he thought of that rather ambiguous phrase ... It was not her hand that he was after. He stopped smiling when he considered what marriage would mean; imprisoned in one of the town's little houses, not for a week or a month or even a year, but forever. Until he died. You could not pack an adobe house onto a horse and move on down the trail. He would grow old here, would wither, chained to one spot like a captured animal. Could he do it? Sometimes, when he was in Elena's captivating presence, he was sure that he could. Other times, when the wind was blowing down out of the mountains from the north, when he was certain that he could detect the grassy odor of the northern plains on that wind, he was not at all sure.

But as he rode back into Los Robles with the other *vaqueros*, introspection was banished from his mind when he remembered that there was going to be a fiesta that evening. He loved the local fiestas; Elena and her people knew how to celebrate. They were always celebrating something: a saint's birthday, a relative's birthday, any excuse for music, dancing, and drinking.

Which was fine with Gabe. After a hard day in the saddle, a fiesta would be a welcome relief. For the past month he'd been working the way no self-respecting Oglala warrior would ever have worked, not even in the hunt, where each man was free to quit when he wanted, to rest, or go home, or to mount and hunt again. It had been the same in war. A warrior was free to quit the fight whenever he tired of it, leaving his comrades to carry on without him. A Lakota warrior did not take orders from any man. Little wonder, then, that the white man's army had won most of the major battles.

Gabe had a room in Don Javier's house. After unsaddling his horse, brushing the animal down, and seeing that it had plenty of feed and water, he went into the house to clean up. He missed having the freedom to plunge himself naked into a stream, to immerse his body in water, as a Lakota would do; they were a clean people. Lakota men and women often bathed together, unashamed. But not the Spanish. Even more than the Anglos, the Spanish had a strange sense of shame concerning their bodies, as if the human body were somehow evil, something to be hidden from one's fellow man, perhaps even from oneself. Gabe had heard the local priest tell his parishioners that this was the law of their God. Yet this very same priest also claimed that his God had personally created the very human bodies that were to be abhorred. Somewhere, in all that tortured reasoning, Gabe suspected there might lurk some small fault of logic.

Gabe had rigged a washing place in an unused laundry room; sponging at himself from a washbasin was not going to get rid of the thick coating of dust that covered his clothing and any bit of exposed skin. After taking off his boots, Gabe walked barefoot to the laundry room, carrying clean clothing. He then went out into the yard to fetch several buckets of water. He passed the old cook on the way. She blushed. Everyone knew what Gabe did in the laundry room.

Closing the door, Gabe stripped, then, after wetting himself with a bucket of water, he soaped himself thoroughly. It was pleasant to feel the soap loosening the grime of his hard day's work. Work that no self-respecting warrior would dream of performing. It was even more pleasant when he slowly poured two more buckets of water over himself, washing away the dirt. He watched the muddy water run along a V-shaped depression in the floor, then disappear through a drain hole cut into one corner of the wall.

As he rinsed himself, Gabe could not help thinking of the coming fiesta. And about Elena. She would be there, standing with the unmarried girls. She would undoubtedly be looking straight at him, as she usually did, her desire for him plain on her lovely face. There would be dancing. He would feel her body brush by his . . .

Looking down, Gabe saw that his thoughts had aroused him. He laughed unselfconsciously. If this were a city, a place where his actions were more likely to go unnoticed, he would go out right now and buy himself a whore. Then, with his desire sated, he would be able to . . .

To what? Ride on out, no longer bound to this place through Elena? He snorted. How the hell could he really know? There were no whores here, none whom he could safely visit without it becoming common gossip throughout the entire village . . . gossip that would hurt Elena.

Gabe's mood had darkened considerably by the time he'd dried himself and put on clean clothing. As he went out into the plaza, where the musicians were warming up, he was feeling just a touch belligerent. A fight would feel good. He watched the men as they drank. How they laughed and joked. He was tempted to do the same, to let the alcohol take him where it might, loosen his mood, but he resisted the temptation, sensing that if he did, way too much trouble would follow.

It grew dark. Torches were lighted, then the dancing started. A terrible burden, this dancing that didn't let a man and woman really touch one another. Gabe saw that Elena was dancing with another man. He watched her pirouette in front of the man, watched her skirts flare, watched the way her eyes shone. Were they shining for that particular man? Why not? He was handsome enough, he was young, and his eyes never left Elena. Or, more hopefully, perhaps Elena's eyes were shining just for the dance. She loved dancing.

The music stopped as the musicians took time out for a drink. Elena, her face flushed, smiled at her partner. Gabe heard the man say something, heard Elena's answering giggle. He felt an icy cold invading his stomach. Was he growing jealous?

Then Elena turned away from the young man and came over to Gabe. "Gabriel," she said, "you have not danced with me tonight."

She was standing very close. Her breasts were nearly touching the front of his shirt. Since she was quite a bit shorter than Gabe, he had to look down at her, down into her eyes, and past her eyes, into the inviting valley between those lovely breasts. How her eyes were shining. Gabe sensed that they were definitely shining for him, and he suddenly felt very good.

When the music began again, they danced. Gabe took Elena's hand, and through the hand, was aware of her entire body, felt its aliveness, its heat and sensuality. Despite the girl's thick, flaring skirt, he could sense the movement of her hips, the partially hidden abandon of the way her body seemed to strain toward him. He noticed the faint sheen of perspiration on Elena's face, the heightened glow of her eyes. Her lips were parted, glistening red. She seemed to be having trouble breathing. "Gabriel," she murmured, her voice huskier than normal, "you have not come to see me lately. Have I done something to offend you?"

"Of course not," he replied. Something wrong? No . . . too many things right. His instincts had been trying to warn him that the girl was a danger to him, a danger to the way he lived. But it was a lot easier to be objective about Elena when he was not looking into the magic of those big brown eyes, when he was not standing so close that all he could think about was the potential softness of her breasts . . .

A commotion broke out on the far side of the dance floor. Two young men were shouting angrily at one another. A girl stood nearby, flushing in embarrassment as she stared down at the ground. All heads turned in that direction. All except Elena's. Gabe felt her fingers tighten around his hand. "Come," she said. "Come with me."

"What?" he replied, turning to look at her.

"Come. No one will notice."

He saw then that she had danced him out to the edge of the firelight, next to a dark opening between two buildings. He also saw how much more rapidly her breasts were rising and falling, how her eyes glittered with excitement. For just an instant a voice of caution whispered inside his head, but it was instantly slaughtered by the voice of the warrior, the inner voice that drove Gabe toward risk and excitement.

No one saw them leave as they slipped away into the darkness between the two buildings, Elena guiding Gabe by the hand. She moved unerringly in the dark, as if she knew every step of the way by heart. She drew him on, past the last of the town's buildings. Unable to see well, Gabe trod carefully, his moccasined feet testing the ground. By now he suspected where she was taking him. Toward the little river that ran by the town.

She led him into a grove of cottonwoods. At first it was very dark; the moon, which was nearly full, had been hiding behind thick clouds for the past half hour. Now the clouds parted, and the moon reappeared. Suddenly the grove was transformed into a place of magic, a world of silvery moonlight, and the blackest of shadows.

Elena led the way to the center of the grove, where there was a small clearing. The moonlight shone down, transfiguring her face. Her eyes seemed huge. Her pupils glittered with reflected light . . . and with something more. "Ah, Gabriel . . ." She sighed. "I have waited so long . . . "

Then she was in his arms, the full length of her body pressed against his, her breasts digging into his lower chest. It was amazing how solid they were; they had always looked so soft. He was both shocked and pleased when he realized that she had parted her legs a little so that one of his thighs quite naturally found its way in between her own. She arched her hips forward. "So long . . . waited so long," Elena murmured, but now it was more a moan than a sigh.

There was absolutely no going back, no shrinking away from what was happening. Gabe's arms tightened around Elena. Her face lifted up toward his own. He felt her lips part as he kissed her, felt the moist heat of her mouth, felt her body strain against his. Clothing began to disappear without much memory of how it had happened. There came a time when Elena was lying on her back on a pile of clothing that had been laid down over a bed of leaves. She lay, naked, the moonlight creating dark mysteries in all her hollow places. Gabe's hands roamed her body, marveling at the softness of her skin, at the firmness of the muscles beneath. She took hold of his hands to stop their roaming. She was panting, whimpering. Was it fear? Fear of what her body was leading her toward? Fear of losing her . . . her what?

Then Gabe remembered how she had guided him to this place with such firmness. Was this something she had done many times before? With the young men of the village?

A surge of wild passion passed through him, a desire to possess her for himself. He lowered himself down onto her. *"Mi amor,"* she murmured, clasping her to him. *"Mi amor."*

He felt heat, a musky wetness, and guided himself into that heat and wetness—or tried to. There was resistance, something was pushing back against him. Elena did not seem to notice. "Please . . . now!" she pleaded.

He pushed, felt the resistance continue, then stretch, and suddenly release, and he was inside her, his jealousy gone. The way her body arched as he entered her, her sharp cry of pain, the resistance itself, told him that what he had earlier thought about Elena, about her being with other men, was not true. He was the first.

And then Elena's hips were surging upward toward his own, reacting, seeking. Her arms tightened around his lower body, eagerly pulling him deeper, deeper, her cries of pain changing to pleased whimpers of triumph.

Inside Gabe's head, male pride struggled with a sense of deep foreboding. But only for a moment; no amount of foreboding could long resist the hot, alive feel of Elena's body quivering beneath him. Crying out inarticulately, he gave her what each of their bodies so desperately desired.

CHAPTER ELEVEN

They tried to hide their affair, but in such a small community, it was next to impossible. Perhaps it was the fulfilled look on Elena's face, or the rather haunted one on Gabe's. Or the growing realization among the townspeople that both of them often disappeared at the same time. Or the leaves and grass that clung to their clothing. Whatever the cause, everyone knew that they were lovers.

Gabe expected immediate problems, but to his amazement they did not materialize. For one thing, Elena was an orphan, without brothers or sisters. Her elderly grandfather didn't seem to be aware of much that went on around him. He spent most of his time growing vegetables and tending his fruit trees. There was no one to claim *venganza*, vengeance. Quite the opposite. As an entity, the village was relieved that Elena seemed to have found herself a man. The village elders, such as Don Javier, were relieved because Elena would not become a charge on the community. The women were relieved because they did not like the idea of a young, beautiful, unattached girl remaining single; it was a threat to their hold over their own men.

The understanding, of course, was that Gabe was going to marry Elena. He could read the expectation on the faces of the townspeople. He could also read their puzzlement that he was taking so long to declare his intentions.

The trap had closed around Gabe. The silken trap. He knew it, he could feel its gossamer fibers, stronger than the hardest steel, pinning him in place, for the trap was inside his own mind, the trap of obligation. It was an obligation to which Gabe was not accustomed. That memorable night in the cottonwood grove down by the river he and Elena had only done that which was natural, a man and a woman, attracted to one another, coupling. As an adolescent, Gabe had done the same with several Lakota girls. It was more or less expected, part of growing up, although once a Lakota woman was married, she was not to be toyed with.

With Elena, the situation was different. In a Lakota camp, there was more of a sense of everyone being one large family. In Los Robles there were many very separate families. A woman could expect to be cared for only by the family into which she was born, or the family into which she married. Since Elena had no family of her own, she must marry or suffer. But now that most precious of all jewels available to a Spanish woman, her maidenhood, had been taken from her. She was no longer eligible for a decent marriage. In local eyes, Gabe had marked her for life, and having done so, was now responsible for that same life.

Which was the trap. Gabe felt an increasing sense of anger as the expectations of the citizens of Los Robles tightened around him. He was painfully aware of Elena's growing puzzlement as day after day passed and he did not ask her to marry him. Looking into those big brown eyes, Gabe knew guilt, an emotion with which he was not particularly familiar. Guilt began to foster resentment, not against himself, but against Elena, and against the people of Los Robles. He'd been sandbagged!

To justify his anger, he began to wonder if Elena, fearing that he might be about to leave the village, had used her body as a lure, had planned to enmesh him permanently, that night she'd taken him down to the cottonwood grove.

His suspicions began to show in his behavior toward Elena. He was increasingly curt and he tended to make acid comments. Elena was not a person to accept slights meekly, she had a strong personality, so she began to return the acid comments. Within a month they were acting a little like an old married couple. They were getting on one another's nerves. In a freer setting, they might have eventually parted quite naturally. But in Los Robles, parting was not considered natural. Worse, if Gabe left Elena now, after having taken from her that jewel greater than all the rubies and diamonds in the world, the precious flower of her virginity, she would be dishonored, ruined, a target of contempt.

And so the tension grew. Not that it kept Gabe and Elena from making love. Each had a hunger and fascination for the other's body that would not be denied. They made love whenever possible, at first mainly in the cottonwood grove, until the town's adolescents, having discovered this trysting place, almost caught them in the act. They found other places farther from town, but were nearly caught several times. Finally, Gabe began to visit Elena at her grandfather's house when the old man was out working with his trees, or when he rode to the next town. Gabe even began smuggling Elena into his room at Don Javier's through a back door. He was sure Don Javier knew, but so far the old man had not interfered. Although that might change. Gabe could see concern growing in Don Javier's eyes. It would only be a matter of time before Don Javier had a little talk with him about his responsibilities.

Gabe and Elena were in his room very early one morning, together in bed, both naked. They had just made love and were catching their breaths when Gabe noticed that it was growing light outside. Normally, Elena returned home before dawn to preserve the fiction that no one really knew what they were doing. It had not worked this time; as Elena was getting ready to leave, Gabe had dragged her back down onto the bed for one last bout of lovemaking, which had turned into another, until all sense of time had deserted them. Now Gabe lay on his side, rather covertly studying Elena, amazed, as usual, by the firm lushness of her body, by the way her breasts thrust straight upward, even though she was lying on her back. He studied the silky, rounded strength of her thighs, the sleekness of her belly, the sated expression of her lovely face. He looked at the dark triangle of hair where her legs joined, noticing its wetness, wetness he had helped put there, and noticing all this, he felt a surge of anger. Each time he made love to Elena, he strengthened

the cage that awaited him. A cage that seemed inevitable.
He felt a pang of undirected, confusing anger. But at whom?
At what?

Suddenly, from outside, came the sound of a horse being
run hard, followed by shouting. Elena's eyes opened wide,
and she clasped the blankets to her naked body. "What is
it?" she whispered.

"I don't know," Gabe replied, listening. More voices
had joined in the shouting. He heard doors slamming, people
running out into the street.

He immediately began to dress. Elena did the same, but
she was still dressing when Gabe went out the door carrying
his Winchester, a pistol thrust into his belt.

When he stepped into the street, it appeared that most of
the town's population was already there, clustered around
a sweaty, dusty horseman. Gabe pushed his way into the
crowd. He saw Don Javier. The old man nodded curtly at
Gabe, whose eyes narrowed. Had there been just a shadow
of contempt in the way Don Javier had looked at him?

Gabe pushed through the crowd. He recognized the horseman; he owned a small ranch about ten miles out of town.

The man was hurt, he was bleeding from a shoulder
wound. "What happened?" Gabe asked Don Javier.

"Apaches," Don Javier replied grimly. "They raided
several homes near where this man lives. He got away . . .
after they killed his wife and son."

"Any others hurt?"

"We don't know. It doesn't sound good. When enough
of us are armed, we're going over there to find out. Are
you coming?"

Gabe breathed in sharply. "Of course!" he snapped.
Before his involvement with Elena, the question would
never have been asked.

He saw her then as he turned to go back to the house and
collect his gear. She had come into the plaza, and although
everyone had piled out of bed in a hurry, her clothing
seemed, at least to him, more disarrayed than anyone else's.
Gabe noticed a few of the younger people looking in her
direction, snickering, talking to one another behind cupped

hands. Burning with anger, he went into the house and armed himself.

Ten minutes later, he rode out with twenty other armed men. It was a grim procession. No one said much. Less than an hour later they arrived at the scene of the raid. The man who had ridden into town with the warning dismounted in front of his house. He got down slowly, his face anguished.

It was not a pretty scene. The house, being adobe, had not burned, but a small barn was in ashes. His wife and son lay dead in front of the house. Both had been scalped. ''They are the lucky ones,'' Don Javier murmured within Gabe's hearing.

Half an hour later, they learned of others less lucky. They had ridden past two more burned houses, with no sign of anyone dead or living, and were approaching a third house when they heard someone call out weakly from behind a pile of boulders. The riders fanned out cautiously. On the far side of the boulders, they found a young man, badly wounded, lying in a pool of his own blood.

Gabe did not think the man would live. But he could still talk. The man told Don Javier and the others how the Apaches had attacked an hour before dawn, how he had been cut off outside, then shot. He'd crawled away among the boulders and had been able to hold off his attackers. But he had not been able to keep the Apaches from killing his father and capturing his older brother and his little sister.

In a steadily weakening voice, the wounded man reported that by the time they'd reached his house, the Apaches had already held several captives. They were, as far as he could ascertain, the Gonzalez children, a little girl about three years old, and her baby brother. There had been a woman, too, although he had not been able to tell who she was. With his older brother and his sister, that made five captives.

The man died a few minutes after he'd finished his account. They placed him inside the wrecked, blood-spattered interior of his house, next to the scalped, mutilated body of his father. There was no time for burial; they had to get on the trail of the Apaches at once. They had to try to save the captives.

They rode as hard as they could without ruining the horses. They rode silently, a group of very grim men. Fortunately, the trail they were following was fairly clear, the Apaches were not making much of an effort to hide their tracks.

They passed another village. More men joined them; by now quite an area had been alerted. "You react very quickly," Gabe said to Don Javier.

The old man shrugged. "We've had a lot of experience over a great many years. Centuries."

"They're old enemies, these Apaches?"

"Yes . . . old. They, and the Navajo, arrived in this part of the world at about the same time we did. They immediately started raiding and killing, both us and the Pueblo Indians. To the Apache, killing is sport. Killing and torturing. Both the Apaches and the Comanches have made life very hard for our people. The Comanches are another tribe who kill for sport. When we find either one, we exterminate them like wild beasts."

Gabe nodded. Even way up in the Dakotas, when he'd still been living with the Oglala, he'd heard of the Apaches. "Enemy" their name meant, and they were the enemy of all, both red man and white, a cruel people who sowed death and terror all around them. They were universally hated. And feared.

The day wore on. As it began to grow dark, it became more difficult to track the Apache raiding party, although they still weren't doing much to hide their tracks. Now Gabe took the lead. His Oglala past had made him a superb tracker, and he followed the trail until it became impossible to do so any longer; it was a very dark night.

They stopped for the night, partly to rest the horses. The men fretted, few of them sleeping, all of them haunted by what must be happening to the captives. In the morning, before it got quite light, they remounted and continued on, tired, bitter, filled with foreboding.

They found the captured woman just before noon. The

trail had been growing fainter and fainter; the ground was quite hard here, and the Apaches now seemed to be making a greater attempt at covering their tracks. Then Gabe spotted, about a mile off to one side, a spiral of descending vultures. He immediately forgot about the faded tracks he was following. "Let's go!" he called out to the others, then kicked his horse into a canter toward the vultures.

The woman had been staked out on the ground, spread-eagled. She was naked. From the way she'd been torn up between the thighs, she'd obviously been raped. Brutally raped. Then mutilated. Then staked out and tortured. Her eyes were missing, along with several finger joints. Her breasts were hacked to ribbons. Yet these wounds were not what had killed her. Her belly had been cut open and she'd been left to die slowly. The men looked down at her body in horror. Her intestines bulged out in shiny coils. The terrible rictus of her mouth indicated that she must have died screaming. She'd been scalped, of course.

The men stood around her corpse, silent, their faces dark with rage and horror. They cut her loose from the stakes, wrapped her in a poncho, and buried her near where she had died. Then they mounted and turned their horses back toward the trail the Apaches had left. Their faces were ugly with the desire to kill.

Gabe looked down at the trail. "They're not so far ahead now," he told Don Javier. "The woman lived for a long time. That's why the vultures hadn't started on her yet. She must have died just a little while before we arrived. The Apaches probably stayed to watch as much of her dying as they dared. Then maybe they saw us coming."

Don Javier nodded woodenly. "That would be their way. Death, painful death, fascinates them."

Gabe nodded curtly. "We'll see how much they enjoy their own death."

Don Javier looked over at Gabe and saw the grim look on his face. He hesitated, then spoke. "You once told me that you were raised by Indians. Doesn't it bother you to ride against other Indians?"

Gabe pondered for a moment. He remembered a certain

amount of cruelty among the Oglala, but never quite what
he had seen today. "These are not like the people I grew
up with," he said shortly. Don Javier, after another look
at Gabe's face, chose not to pursue the matter.

They found the little girl late in the day. At first Gabe
thought that it was a piece of cloth caught on a tree limb,
perhaps an effort by the remaining captives to alert anyone
who might be following. Then, as he drew closer, Gabe
saw that it was not just a piece of cloth. So did the men
with him. "*Aiiyyy . . . Santa Maria,*" he heard one of them
mutter under his breath.

The girl was about three years old. She'd been pinned to
the tree trunk by the simple expedient of slamming her body
against a projecting piece of broken limb. The limb had
entered her back up high, between the shoulder blades, and
was protruding from her chest just beneath collarbone level.
And she was still alive. Just barely. As Gabe and Don Javier
rode up, the little girl's eyes, which had been nearly closed,
slowly opened, first in terror, as if she believed that her
killers were returning, then in hope, when she saw that it
was her own people.

But it was far too late. Even as the men were trying to
decide how to pull her off that bloody piece of broken
branch, the girl died.

They buried her. By the time the last of the dirt had been
shoveled over her small corpse, several of the men were
half-mad with the desire to kill. Gabe was impressed by
Don Javier's calm, and commented on it. The old man
shrugged wearily. "I have lived with this all my life."

Several of the men wanted to ride on at once. Gabe
disagreed. "I think they killed the girl because they knew
we were getting too close. They knew that finding her would
slow us down, maybe even convince us not to continue
following. If we follow, they'll probably kill all the other
captives so that they can ride on more quickly."

"You're suggesting that we abandon the chase, then?"
one man asked angrily.

Gabe shook his head. "No. Just make them think that

we are. Better yet, we'll make them think we've lost their trail.''

"They'll get away," the man insisted bitterly.

Gabe almost smiled, although, in the light of the day's horror, smiling was not easy. "No," he said softly. "They won't."

By now every man was hanging on to his words. "The only way they can go," Gabe said, glancing toward a range of hills about a mile away, "the only way that would make sense to me, is for them to head up through that pass. No! Don't look in that direction!" he warned the men. "They may be watching."

He then told them how he intended following along the base of the hills, as if they had lost the Apaches' trail and were riding on blind, hoping to run across it again. Then they would spring his trap. "Because once they think we're off in the wrong direction, they'll . . . stop to have a little fun again."

The men nodded grimly. There was a little more discussion, but all of them eventually agreed to Gabe's plan. They rode out a few minutes later, trying to look as lost as possible. It was, by then, quite late in the day, and darkness soon overtook them. Blessed, covering darkness.

They now veered off to the right, toward a canyon that Gabe had noticed when he'd been considering his plan. This particular canyon appeared to intersect the pass he'd noticed, about halfway up into the mountains. They found the canyon easily enough, although riding up it quietly was made difficult by the dark. However, as Gabe had already noted, these men were superb riders. They made good time, and in relative silence.

The canyon's connection to the broader pass was not easy to locate, but by now the moon had risen, and Gabe was able to find the narrow, rock-and-brush-choked passageway that would lead them in.

They entered the pass about a mile above the Apache camp. They could see a small fire below them, well hidden, but hidden only from below, from out on the plain, where the Apaches believed them to be. "Good," Gabe murmured to Don Javier. "They're overconfident."

The hunters fanned out, beginning a careful approach toward the raiders' camp. Their caution was almost wrecked by a horrible scream that came from the camp. A man's scream. Gabe sensed the men around him straining to kick their horses into a gallop and ride straight in, but he restrained them. "Too soon," he whispered. "They'll kill the captives and escape."

They approached the camp under tight discipline, still too quickly for Gabe, but fortunately, hideously, the man's screams covered the sound of their approach. They were only about a hundred yards away when they got their first clear glimpse into the camp. Gabe counted thirteen Apaches. They were short, thickset men, with black, greasy hair cut short over their faces and hanging down long behind. They wore a motley combination of buckskins and white man's clothing. They were armed, but most of their weapons were lying stacked against rocks or trees, while the majority of the Apaches crowded in around the man they were torturing.

They'd tied him between two trees, held up by rawhide thongs tied around his wrists. The man was sagging between the tree trunks, his body bucking and jerking as an Apache stood in front of him, slowly peeling away skin from his upper chest. They'd already partially skinned his forearms. Bloody pieces hung in long strips.

Gabe looked around for the other captives; there should be two more. He saw them then; a small boy, crouching, terrified, as he watched the torture. The girl, perhaps thirteen or fourteen years old, had been backed up against a boulder. Three Apaches were closing in on her, grinning, obviously about to start a rape. The girl had burn blisters on her face and bare shoulders; obviously she had not had an easy time of it. So far, her captors had only been toying with her, burning her with brands from the fire. They had raped the older woman right away, leaving the younger, prettier one for later. Dessert. They'd killed the little girl, because girls who were too young to rape were of small value. They'd kept the man for leisurely torture, to see how long it would take him to die. The little boy they would keep alive indefinitely, in the hopes of making him an Apache. Boys had value. They could become warriors.

Gabe saw that the Apaches had been careless in their choice of a campsite. Sheer rock walls blocked off any retreat to the rear. He deployed the men in an arc in front of the camp. When the arc closed in, there would be no way out for the Apaches.

He had the men dismount. Then, accompanied by the screams of the man being skinned, they started toward the camp, a heavily armed semicircle of grim avengers.

The Apache with the skinning knife went first. A bullet from Gabe's Winchester broke his back. The flat boom of the shot was the signal for the rest of Don Javier's men to rush in, firing, killing, screaming their hate.

One of the Apaches tried to kill the girl, but was cut down before he could reach her. It all happened very quickly, Apaches falling, shot, dying. One of them got to his rifle in time to get off a shot that grazed one of the attackers, but then he, too, went down in a hail of lead.

Several Apaches tried to run, only to come up against the sheer stone wall at the rear of the camp. They stood at bay, their faces tense, looking about for a means of escape. There were none. When the Apaches realized their helplessness, they did not plead or whine, but stood erect, stolidly awaiting their fate.

It came more slowly than it might have, but not nearly as slowly as the torture they had meted out to their own captives. Don Javier's men began firing. Bullets plowed into the Apaches, but not all fell, and Gabe saw that Don Javier's men, in their rage and anger, were shooting wildly, missing as often as they hit, and when they hit, they hit badly.

Gabe saw one Apache go down, his groin shot away. Another had one arm nearly blown off, but seemed otherwise unhit. Within seconds, all were hit somewhere, most were down, and the Spaniards were howling with blood lust.

Suddenly, Don Javier's voice rang out. *"¡Basta!"* he

shouted. "Enough! We will not act like wild beasts."

He signaled to one of the men, one of the steadiest, and drawing their pistols, Don Javier and the man he had chosen walked up to the wounded Apaches. Working systematically, they fired killing shots into each Apache. In less than a minute, all were dead.

Reloading his smoking pistol, Don Javier turned toward Gabe. "You see, Gabriel," he said quietly, "it is simply a matter of extermination. One does not torture the rattlesnake that bites his child. There is no question of vengeance. He simply kills the snake so that it will not bite again."

CHAPTER TWELVE

They camped for the night farther down the canyon; no one among them wanted to stay near the Apache camp, with its dead and its hideous memories. The camp they made was a silent camp. The rescued girl seemed numb, and the little boy was too young to really figure it all out. The man who'd been tortured was in great pain, but so grateful over being rescued that he was almost cheerful. The skin that had been partially peeled from his arms and chest had been put back in place. With luck, it would grow again. He would be horribly scarred, but alive.

They started back for Los Robles the next morning. Despite the partial success of their mission, spirits were low. Each man was remembering the raped, butchered woman and the little girl hanging on the tree. It had been decided to leave them where they were buried; it would be too painful for their families to see just how they had died.

As they rode back, Gabe thought over Don Javier's emotionless statement about killing snakes, and the more he thought about it, the more he realized how unlikely it was that red man and white would ever understand one another. There had been too much death, a never-ending round of atrocity. It was all so haphazard. Drunken whites would kill some Indians or rape their women. In retaliation, Indians would raid some outlying settlements, killing and torturing. Then the Army would attack Indians of a completely different tribe than the ones who'd done the raiding, storming into the camp at dawn, murdering men, women, and children. It went on and on, Indians torturing captives, white men making tobacco pouches from the breasts of Indian women they'd raped and killed. There were too many differences, two completely dissimilar ways of life. Unable to understand one another, and in their lack of understanding, they were able only to satisfy themselves with hatred and death.

By the time they reached Los Robles, Gabe had made some decisions. There seemed no room left for him in either the white man's world or the red. However, these people, the people of Don Javier's village, appeared to live somewhere in between those two other worlds, those warring worlds of which Gabe owned only fragments. Perhaps it was his fate to find the end of his wanderings in the world of Los Robles. He had ridden out with its men, had fought alongside them, and they now shared the bond of mutual danger. Perhaps he could now completely join them, perhaps he could now think of them as his own people.

Gabe had been back in Los Robles for only a few hours when he asked Elena if she would marry him. He saw the way her eyes shone as she accepted. He also saw how beautiful she was, how sensual, what a good companion she would make. Why, then, Gabe asked himself, did he feel so uneasy? As if a huge iron door had slammed shut, imprisoning him inside a dark and dangerous place.

The wedding was to be held in two months. The village priest insisted on the delay; he wanted time to instruct Gabe in the details of the Catholic religion. He refused to marry them unless Gabe joined the church. Gabe didn't mind. To him, one white man's religion was pretty much like another.

Gabe continued to work the herds with the other men. He no longer chafed at the permanency of this kind of life. He no longer felt much of anything. A soothing numbness had stolen over him. He did not fight it.

He and Elena still met secretly, but now there was a numbness even in their lovemaking. The old excitement was gone. Gabe wondered if this is how it would be through all the years they were married; not unpleasant, but . . . lacking the excitement that had so far filled his life. Perhaps it was better that way. Perhaps it was time to live the way other men lived.

Then renewed excitement came to the village. One day Ramon returned from Santa Fe. "We're in trouble," he told Don Javier.

Don Javier and Gabe had been sitting together in Don Javier's living room when Ramon came in. Both men could see from the look on Ramon's face that the trouble must be severe.

"It's the Ring," Ramon explained. "They've bribed that crooked territorial legislature to pass a new law . . . to break up the old land grants."

Gabe saw Don Javier stiffen in his chair. "But they can't do that! The federal government will have to step in. It's against the treaty! The Treaty of Guadalupe Hidalgo clearly states that—"

Ramon laughed bitterly. "Those thieves in Washington have no use for any treaty that doesn't make them richer. They'll approve whatever the people who pay them the biggest bribes tell them to approve. To them, any treaty is only paper. Ask the Indians what treaties are worth in this country."

"What's happening?" Gabe asked, not understanding.

Don Javier shrugged his shoulders and sighed. He looked confused. Apaches and Texans he was willing to fight, but apparently the thieves in Washington and Santa Fe were more than he could handle.

Ramon took up the slack. "New Mexico used to be part of Old Mexico," he told Gabe. "Until 1847, when the war between Mexico and the United States took away about a third of Mexico's territory. The treaty that ended the war, the Treaty of Guadelupe Hidalgo, made a stipulation that all the old Spanish land grants would be honored by the United States."

"And of course, they weren't," Gabe murmured.

"It's never been that simple," Ramon replied. "In many instances they have been honored, but bit by bit, using every crooked trick they can dream up, speculators have been stealing the land from its original owners. In California, bankers talked the big Spanish landowners into accepting loans, and when they couldn't repay those loans—they were cash poor—the banks took their lands away. In New Mexico it's been a little more difficult. Here, many of the old Spanish grants were made not to individuals, but to communities. For instance, most of the land around Los Robles is owned by the Pueblo, to be used communally by all of us. So far, that's made it hard to steal. But now this new law says that any person who has even the smallest stake in any land grant can challenge the entire grant. Then the grant can be parceled up and sold off to the highest bidders. That means that if someone can bribe some local drunk to sell his share of the land grant to them, they can challenge it and force it into a sale. And since most of the papers and records are in the hands of the speculators, they will, in most cases, be the only ones who bid.''

"Why do they have the papers?" Gabe asked.

"Because they control the governor, and through him, the archives. The ones that are left. The governor had most of the old records 'accidentally' burned. Hundreds of years of deeds and legal decisions were used to start fires in private stoves, so we have very few original documents left to prove what is ours and what isn't.''

Gabe said nothing for a moment. Here it was, all over again, the corrupt and greedy, men who could never seem to accumulate enough, stealing from those who did the actual work. And stealing it with the help of an equally corrupt government. "Who are these men?" he asked.

Ramon's face was bleak when he answered. "A group of speculators with headquarters in Santa Fe. They're called the Ring. The Santa Fe Ring. Everybody who's not one of them, or bribed by them, hates them. Even plenty of Anglos hate them, because they steal from the Anglos, too.''

"Perhaps several of us should visit the men who make up this 'Ring,' '' Gabe said quietly. "And see if they value their lives more than your . . . our land.''

Ramon shook his head. "If we just rode in and shot them up, a war would follow. We wouldn't be able to stand that. They have the weight of the government behind them.

They'd send in troops, start hanging people . . ."

Now Don Javier broke in. "But those *hijos de putas* would be dead," he said grimly. "And even if I were to hang, I would feel better because of their deaths. We've put up with their thievery far too long . . ."

"No, Don Javier," Ramon insisted. "There's another way, a better way. Through the law. Or else why did you send me back east to study gringo law? I can use every trick of that law to delay them, to make their lives difficult, to make them want to leave us alone."

"You put too much trust in your law, in laws made to serve our enemies."

"What else do men have except the law?" Ramon demanded, exasperated.

Don Javier glanced toward the wall, where his rifle hung on wooden pegs. "Plenty," he said curtly.

However, after consultation with other village leaders, it was decided to give Ramon a chance to try it his way. Clearly exhilarated by the challenge, the young lawyer threw himself into his task with great vigor. Most of his time was spent in Santa Fe, filing writs, injunctions, and lawsuits. From time to time he returned to Los Robles with progress reports. They were not encouraging. "They've filed against our community grant," he informed the local council. "The land is to be sold off. I've filed a restraining order and countersuit. That should tie them up for a long time."

But not as long a time as Ramon had hoped. Within another two weeks the sale had been made . . . without the local population having been notified. The people of Los Robles suddenly discovered that they were no longer masters of the lands that they had always believed were their own, lands that had been part of their patrimony for more than two hundred fifty years.

"They're drawing up papers that will dispossess us," Ramon reported on his next visit.

"What do these papers matter to us?" one of the younger men asked him.

"When they serve each of us with those papers, when

they put them into our hands," Ramon replied, "then we will no longer own the land."

"It's simple, then," another man cried out. "We won't take the papers!"

"Then they'll throw them at our feet," Ramon said tiredly. "And that will be enough."

"Why should we pay attention to someone else's papers?" the same man shot back.

Ramon shrugged bitterly. "Because they will have the entire weight of the law behind them."

"Then what use is your law to us?"

Ramon did not reply. Gabe noticed how haggard he looked. There were huge dark circles beneath his eyes. His shoulders now slumped a great deal for such a young man. But they suddenly straightened. "The sheriff has to deliver the papers," he said. "And since he's one of us, he'll never agree to do it."

True enough, the sheriff, the same man who'd helped save Gabe from hanging, refused to have anything to do with serving the odious papers. That cheered everyone . . . until Ramon's next visit, when he informed the town council that the governor had signed an order removing the sheriff from his office . . . and appointed another man in his place. "You won't believe this," he told Gabe. "He appointed John Slaughter's old foreman . . . Harrison. I'm sure Harrison won't mind serving us with the eviction notice."

"Harrison!" Gabe burst out.

"Yes. He quit his job with Slaughter and asked to be made sheriff. We don't have to wonder why. It seems that Harrison hasn't forgotten what he owes Los Robles—and you. Be careful, Gabe. Harrison would do anything to see you hang."

Gabe passed his hand over his chin. "I'm beginning to think that Harrison is a man who's lived way too long."

"Wait!" Ramon burst out, alarmed. "Not that way! I still have a few things left that I can do."

And for a while his way worked. Through some brilliant legal maneuvers, Ramon succeeded in getting the writs temporarily revoked. There was jubilation in Los Robles. Ramon was the man of the hour.

But there were also warnings. A friendly Anglo rancher rode into town one day. "I thought I'd better let you know," he said to Ramon. "The Ring has called in Pinkerton gunmen. They know you're the fly in their soup. No tellin' what they might do."

Ramon shrugged off the warning. "They wouldn't dare," he insisted.

"I wouldn't count on that," the rancher replied grimly, then rode out of town.

Gabe took the warning more seriously. Pinkerton gunmen had been hired by more than one greedy man to get rid of opponents. The Pinks stood for the establishment; they would not hesitate to wipe out a little-known Latin lawyer from an insignificant Spanish-speaking pueblo. Not if he stood in the way of men who were ready to pay the agency a big fee.

Gabe tried to reinforce the warning, but Ramon continued to laugh it off. He was still smiling when he left Los Robles, headed for the county seat, where he intended filing more papers. Gabe watched as Ramon rode out of town. Elena was standing beside him. "I should be riding with him," he said.

"You can't!" Elena burst out, alarmed. "That man, Harrison, is there. He has the law behind him. You know he'd kill you if he got the chance."

"I should still go with Ramon," Gabe repeated stubbornly.

Elena put her arms around his neck. "I'd die if anything happened to you," she whispered into his ear. "Don't worry about Ramon. He'll be all right."

When Gabe still resisted, she rather artfully pressed her breasts against his arm. "You worry too much," she murmured against his neck. "Worry about me instead. Worry about how we're going to get inside your room without anyone seeing us."

And faced with the prospect of a very pleasant day, Gabe temporarily forgot about Ramon. Something he would regret for a long time.

CHAPTER THIRTEEN

It was a two-hour ride to the county seat. For those two hours, Ramon was barely conscious of the trip. The land slid by unseen; the real landscape was inside Ramon's head: the land around Los Robles and the stratagems he would have to devise to save it for his people.

He knew deep inside that it was probably a losing battle. His stratagems could delay, but were unlikely to completely stop the powerful forces working against the town. When he'd gone back east to study law, he'd soon become aware of the vast power of the political and business machine that ran the country. Ever since the Civil War, the government had been run by unbelievably corrupt Republican administrations. Ramon wondered what the founder of the Republican party, Abraham Lincoln, would have thought had he lived to see what it had become after his death. No, even before his death. The corruption among thieving war contractors during the fighting had been awe-inspiring. Lincoln, totally absorbed by the war effort, had been able to do little to stop it.

A tragedy that Lincoln had been cut down before he was able to stop the rot. If he'd have been able to. Greed was a terrible enemy. Greed and prejudice. Ramon remembered the many snubs his somewhat darker skin had earned him back east at school, how his people had been referred to as "savages." A people who'd been old in this land before George Washington was even born.

But like it or not, his people were now a part of the

United States. They would have to work out their future
within the framework of its laws. And what laws they were!
To Ramon, the U.S. Constitution and the Bill of Rights
were the most beautiful documents ever written. They held
out a promise of equality for all, a promise of true freedom
. . . as long as individual people fought to preserve those
rights from the greedy who would do all they could to
undermine them.

That was one of the main reasons Ramon had studied
law; so that he would be able to protect otherwise helpless
people. He loved the law, and loved every moment of his
studies. He loved the work he was doing to save his people's
patrimony. What more worthwhile work could a man do?

But what a battle to realize the fruits of the Constitution.
There seemed to be an inexhaustible supply of greedy men,
ready to lie, cheat, steal, and kill in contravention of those
noble promises. How ironic that the United States, the first
nation to throw off the yoke of royalty and inherited titles,
a nation that had, for the first sixty or seventy years of its
existence, been regarded as a revolutionary example, the
hope of the world's politically oppressed, should now be
oppressing his own people so heavily.

Yet, the very laws of the oppressors were there to help
his people. And Ramon would use those laws to the utmost.

He rode into the county seat, filled with resolve. Today
he intended to file at the local courthouse a challenge to
Harrison's appointment as sheriff. That should stir up some
excitement. Might even get him killed. Ramon was not so
foolish that he was ready to completely disregard the possibility that there were men out to kill him. Large amounts
of money were at stake, and there were such men who would
stop at nothing where money was concerned. Such a strange
sickness . . . money valued over life.

The town was its usual sleepy self. Ramon checked his
horse into the local livery stable; he would not be riding
out until the next day. Tonight he would stay here in town
with a family he knew.

He was on his way into the courthouse when he ran into

Harrison, who was on his way out. "Good afternoon, Harrison," Ramon said curtly.

"You call me Sheriff, greaser," Harrison snarled.

"If I considered you the sheriff, I would," Ramon retorted.

A spasm of anger twisted Harrison's features. "By God . . ."

Ramon saw that Harrison had deteriorated since being appointed sheriff. Before, he'd been a lean, hard man, toughened by work. Now, he'd traded his fitness for an easy life. He was growing a gut, and his breath stank of whiskey.

But he was still a dangerous man, and for a moment Ramon thought that Harrison might attack him. However, after a moment's obvious internal struggle, Harrison managed to regain at least a small measure of control over himself. After all, Ramon was an officer of the very court in which they were standing. "I'll see you in hell," Harrison snarled, then left, brushing by Ramon so closely that his shoulder knocked Ramon aside.

Now it was Ramon's turn to risk losing his temper. His pride, and he had a lot of it, made him want to follow after Harrison, to grab him by the shoulder, spin him around, and make him apologize.

But he must not. As tempting as personal violence might be, it was so much more effective to use the power of the law to put men like Harrison in their place.

Ramon spent the rest of the afternoon in the courthouse drawing up documents. Tomorrow morning, when he was satisfied that the documents were correct in every way, he would file for Harrison's removal as sheriff. The governor had claimed that the old sheriff, the one the people had elected, had not filed his bond. That was not true; Ramon himself had helped file that bond, but the paperwork had been conveniently "lost" after reaching Santa Fe. All that should be necessary would be to prove that the bond had been good, and Ramon now had the papers to prove it. Even a man as corrupt as the governor would not be able to refuse the kind of evidence Ramon was about to produce.

When Ramon finally left the courthouse, the sun was

low, nearly ready to move behind the rooftops. He realized that he was very hungry. He decided to go to the town's single restaurant and have something to eat. The family with whom he intended staying was poor; he didn't want to burden them with the extra expense of feeding him.

As he walked along the boardwalk, he was vaguely aware of two other men walking along together on the opposite side of the street. Ramon realized that they were looking straight at him. They were both Anglos, big men, whose clothes were not the clothes of working men, but not quite the clothes of bankers or clerks, either. Both men wore dark, well-cut suits and expensive Stetsons. And guns. One wore crossed gun belts, the other a single gun belt, which drooped low on the right side.

They were still looking at him, meeting his gaze boldly. Ramon instinctively quickened his pace. Unfortunately, the restaurant was on the far side of the street. The same side as the two men. Ramon considered skipping his meal, but his pride, his *orgullo*, his *machismo* would not permit such a loss of face. Crossing the street, he passed directly behind the two men and entered the restaurant. He noticed that both turned to look at him as he passed by.

Ramon had eaten in this particular restaurant many times. He and the proprietor were quite friendly. But tonight, instead of giving Ramon his usual welcoming smile, the proprietor wrung his hands nervously. "Ramon," he said. "I don't think you should—"

"I'm hungry, Juan," Ramon said curtly. "Has your wife made another batch of those wonderful tamales?"

"Oh yes . . . and some *chile verde*, with a sauce that would strip leather off a saddle. But, Ramon, there are men in town . . . "

Ramon pushed on past and sat down at his usual table. Just as he was pulling his chair closer to the table, the little bell over the front door tinkled. Ramon looked up. The two strangers were coming in through the doorway. They stopped for a moment and surveyed the room. When they spotted Ramon, their eyes locked onto him. He felt his stomach twist. The way they were looking at him . . .

The restaurant's owner approached the two men. "*Señores*?" he said hesitantly.

One of the men turned toward Juan. The other kept his eyes on Ramon. The one facing Juan asked, "You got anything in this dump fit for a white man to eat?"

Juan's face tightened. He did not like being insulted. "*Señores . . .*" he murmured, his voice slightly hoarse.

Then the second man spoke. "Look what's settin' over there, Ned," he said in a nasal twang. "A greaser. I don't eat with no greasers."

The first man, Ned, turned his stare back onto Ramon. "I'll be damned," he said. His speech was not nearly as crude as the other man's. "A greaser dressed up like a white man. Trying to pass."

They were both facing Ramon now. He noticed the heavy gold watch chain that crossed over the front of Ned's vest. He was obviously prospering. A prosperous killer. Because that was undoubtedly what the two men were, the Pinkerton killers he'd been warned about.

Ramon felt a spasm of disgust. Pinkertons. From the bad side of the Pinkerton Agency. There were other Pinkerton Agents, good men, who daily risked their lives battling bandits, thieves, and killers. But not these particular Pinkertons. They were simply hired gunmen.

While studying law, Ramon had been fascinated by the history of the Pinkerton National Detective Agency. It had been founded back in the fifties by a young Scottish immigrant, Allan Pinkerton. At the time, the United States was in the midst of a wave of criminal activity. Like the English, the Americans had resisted the founding of regular police forces, fearing that the police would be used to suppress the liberties of the people, as was the case in continental Europe. The cities were hotbeds of crime. Private guards were the only real protection, but only the rich were able to afford them. It was even worse out on the frontier, where a man was expected to be his own law or die.

Pinkerton, a powerfully built, intelligent young man, had, after moving to Chicago, personally apprehended a local bandit. Bare handed. The resulting notoriety had impressed the young Scot. Aware of the lack of law, he founded his famous agency. For years he'd thrown fear into bandits and killers all over the United States. As his fame grew, his Pinkerton National Detective Agency developed into an organization of impressive power and efficiency. Its rogues' gallery tracked the activities of lawbreakers from coast to coast. Its small army of agents worked everywhere, much of the time undercover, unmasking criminals, and either bringing them in to stand trial or killing them when they resisted.

During the war, Allan Pinkerton had provided protection for the new president, Abraham Lincoln. He had run spies into the Confederacy. And when the war was over, the Pinkerton Agency was more powerful than ever.

Maybe it was the power that had done it. The power and the wealth and the new respectability, the patronage of the rich, of the movers and doers. The agency was a perfect instrument, with its undercover operators, for protecting the commercial empires of the rich against any encroachments by the people who worked for them.

Or perhaps it was the second generation of Pinkertons. Old Allan had had a terrible stroke several years earlier, which effectively took him out of the daily operation of the agency, leaving it to his two sons, Robert and William. Sons who had grown up wealthy, used to the exercise of power. Men who operated on a par with the robber barons who ran the country.

The older branch of the agency remained; the fearless, relentless detectives who were the scourge of bank robbers and assassins. But another branch had been formed, the Pinkerton guards, who were hired to protect property, to smash strikes, to drive small men off land that big men wanted. They were hired thugs and killers, scum of the earth. Like the two Pinkertons who now faced Ramon.

How ironic, Ramon thought, that old man Pinkerton had been run out of Britain for labor agitation, that he had been a member of the Underground Railroad, that he'd helped escaped slaves along their route to the North and freedom.

How much did the old man really know about men like Ned and his companion?

What did it matter? Ramon knew that he was in big trouble. These two men would kill him with no more emotion than squashing a bug. He was unarmed, but that would not stop them from shooting him down. With the weight of the agency behind them, with fat William Pinkerton probably having sent them himself, they were, in effect, above the law.

They started toward Ramon, fanning out a little. "Don't you hear well, greaser?" Ned was saying. "We don't share our eating space with savages."

Ned's right hand was slowly sliding down his side toward his pistol. Ramon saw that the bottom of the holster had been tied to Ned's thigh, to help the pistol slide from it with greater ease. Ramon was also aware of a terrible dryness inside his own throat, of a pounding in his chest. If only he had not left his pistol in his saddlebags!

And then the bell over the door tinkled again. A moment later a family came into the restaurant, an Anglo family; a mother, a father, two little boys, and a girl just entering puberty. Unaware of the impending drama, they spread out into the room, chattering gaily, looking for a place to sit. Ned and his companion hesitated. The two little boys were between themselves and Ramon.

Ramon quickly stood up, then walked straight by the two Pinkertons. They turned to follow . . . and ran into the family's father and mother. While they milled together, Ramon walked out into the street, and once outside, slipped down an alley and headed straight toward the livery stable.

His saddlebags were hanging on one of the low side walls of the stall that held his horse. He reached inside one of the bags and pulled out his pistol, an old cap-and-ball Remington .44. The saddlebags also held an extra loaded cylinder. He took out the cylinder, too, and slipped it into his coat pocket.

The pistol went into his belt. He was moving toward his horse gear, ready to saddle and bridle his mount and ride out of town, when he was aware of movement near the livery stable's big sliding doors.

It was Ned and the other Pinkerton. They were moving down the street, straight toward the stable. There was no way Ramon could ride out now, even bareback. The only way out of the livery stable big enough to pass a horse was through those front doors. He'd have to ride straight past the two gunmen.

Leaving his horse and gear, Ramon moved back into the murky interior of the livery stable. Confident that he could not be seen, he slipped out a small side door. After the dim interior of the stables, the outside light nearly blinded him. As soon as he could see clearly, he scanned his surroundings, looking for the Pinkertons. They were nowhere in sight. He imagined them, carefully working their way through the murky interior of the livery stable, hunting.

Maybe he should have stayed inside. With lots of cover, he would have had a better chance than out here in the open. Too late for that now.

He walked quickly through the town, wondering what to do. Perhaps he should take refuge with a local Spanish family. But that would only expose other people to danger; they would want to help him. He was not about to place honest people in jeopardy from professional killers.

And then there was his pride. He did not like to run. But the odds were so much against him. How he wished Gabe were here. A strange man, Gabe Conrad, with his half-Indian ways. But a good man, an honest man, and one hell of a man to have on your side in a fight.

He should never have come here alone. Too late now. Then he had an idea. Why not go to the courthouse? It might make the Pinkertons think a little . . . killing a man, an attorney, an officer of the court, inside the courthouse itself.

Walking fast, Ramon was halfway down the street, heading toward the courthouse, when another man stepped out onto the boardwalk directly in his path. Harrison.

Ramon altered his course, intending to walk around the obstruction. Harrison stepped sideways, blocking his route. "Get out of my way, Harrison," Ramon snapped.

"You just hold it right there, greaser," Harrison replied. "I notice you got a gun stuck in your belt. I don't allow guns in my town. Hand it over."

Ramon's right hand moved closer to his gun butt. "Harrison, if you don't get out of my way, I'll blow your guts out. If you're serious about disarming someone, start with those two Pinkerton bastards."

Harrison hesitated. So far, he had not taken Ramon seriously. Just a little greaser lawyer. Now, aware of the look on Ramon's face, the look of a man ready to kill, Harrison prudently took a step backward.

Then he smiled. "You mean . . . those two gents?"

Ramon was aware that Harrison was looking past him, over his shoulder. He hated to face away from Harrison, but he had little choice. Turning, he saw the two Pinkertons bearing down on him. They were only about forty yards away and coming on fast.

As far as Ramon was concerned, Harrison no longer existed. He turned to face the two Pinkertons. They stopped about ten yards away. For a moment, neither Pinkerton moved. Ramon wondered if they would do the obvious, step down into the street and spread out, making two separate, harder-to-hit targets.

He saw the illiterate one looking to his right, into the street. Maybe the best plan of action would be to let the Pinkertons start in that direction, then draw his pistol and start shooting while they were still close together, not quite ready. Shoot as fast as he could, empty the cylinder, and hope that his bullets hit flesh.

Ramon had little doubt that they'd kill him, that he was a dead man. But maybe he'd kill at least one of them. Maybe cripple them both. Then his death would not be a total waste. He had a moment's regret that he had not had time to file his legal papers. Far too late for that now. "Señores," he said softly, reaching for his pistol, knowing that he was just a split second earlier than either of the Pinkertons. They had not expected him to start the fight.

The bullet hit Ramon unexpectedly. It hit him very hard. He felt it slam into his body, stunning him, and he knew that he was falling. How had it happened? He'd been certain that he'd be able to draw and get off at least one shot before either of the Pinkertons had a chance to fire, but his gun had not yet completely left the waistband of his trousers when the bullet hit him.

Then he realized that the bullet had come from behind, that it was his back that had felt the blow, and that he was falling forward, not backward.

Harrison! It was Harrison's bullet! Harrison had shot him in the back!

Even before he hit the hard, splintery surface of the boardwalk, more bullets were plowing into Ramon's body. Pinkerton bullets. The two gunmen had drawn by now, and were firing steadily, shooting him to pieces. Strange that the bullets did not hurt, but merely shook him. He was aware of their impact against his flesh, of the way they were tearing him up inside, but instead of pain, there was only a hideous numbness.

The terrible noise of the guns finally stopped. It was very quiet now. Such peace. Ramon was aware that he was lying on his face. He saw an ant crawling across dirty wood not more than six inches from his face. He tried to move. After a considerable struggle, he was able to raise his head a little.

He saw his pistol, lying on the boardwalk only a couple of feet away. He started to reach for it, but discovered that his hand and arm were not eager to obey. And now the first of the pain came, a jolt of agony that made him suck in his breath.

He gritted his teeth and tried again. He could see his hand inching toward the fallen pistol. Could also see a pair of shiny, expensive-looking boots positioned very close to the pistol. He saw one of the boots draw back, then kick his pistol out of sight.

Then the boots were moving toward him. One hooked underneath his shoulder, then shoved, turning him over onto his back. "*Aaaaahhhh!*" Ramon cried out as terrible pain surged through his ruined body.

"Goddamn," he heard one of the Pinkertons say. "This greaser can soak up one hell of a lot of lead."

Ramon was aware of legs straddling his body. Like tree trunks. He looked up those legs, up past a vest with a shiny watch chain. It was the one called Ned. Ned was holding something in his hand. A pistol. That's what it was, a revolver. Ramon had not at first recognized the object for a pistol because of the foreshortening. The pistol was aimed straight at his face; he was staring up the huge hole in the muzzle. Ramon heard the awful multiple click as Ned pulled the hammer back into full-cock position.

"So long, asshole," he heard Ned say. The voice seemed to be coming from far, far away. But the voice was not what was important. What mattered was the way Ned's trigger finger was whitening as it applied pressure against the trigger.

And then, for Ramon, the world exploded into terminal darkness.

CHAPTER FOURTEEN

Ramon's body reached Los Robles early the next day. It was brought in by two young men from the family with whom Ramon had intended to spend the night. They arrived with the body draped across the back of a mule, arms and legs dangling, hair matted with blood, flies buzzing around oozing bullet holes.

Gabe was in his room when the body arrived. The first he knew of it was the sound of wailing out in the street. Picking up his rifle, he went outside. Even before he saw the body, he had a premonition as to what he would find.

Relatives were taking Ramon from the back of the mule. The body slipped and thudded into the dust. Everyone gasped. Most of Ramon's face had been shot away.

Gabe moved closer. He was aware of Elena, standing next to him. "I told you I should have gone with him," he said to her, his face bleak. She flinched and looked away.

The two young men who had brought the body recounted the events of the previous evening. An old woman had seen the whole thing from an upstairs window. She'd told them, and half the town, how Harrison had shot Ramon in the back, and how one of the others, one of the Pinkerton men, had rolled Ramon over and shot him in the face.

"Harrison," Gabe murmured under his breath. "I should have killed him a long time ago."

He went back to his room and began to collect his gear. He was rolling and tying his trail bedding when he heard a slow, hesitant knocking on the door. He opened it. Elena was standing in the hallway, hands clasped in front of her body, head down, waiting. When he said nothing, she lifted her head. "I did this, didn't I?" she asked in a very soft voice.

"Did what?"

"Stopped you from going with Ramon. From helping him. In a way, I suppose I helped kill him."

Gabe saw that the girl's big brown eyes were filled with a mixture of fear and sadness. Yes, he'd been feeling anger toward her, anger over her interference, for the way she'd weakened his sense of duty by offering the lure of her body. But, aware of her misery, his anger turned to compassion. "I'm a grown man, Elena," he said gently. "It's my responsibility whether or not I do something. Don't think badly of yourself."

She nodded, still looking rather unconvinced. She'd lowered her head, but now she looked up again, and he could see the fear in her eyes. "You're going, aren't you. You're going to kill the men who shot Ramon."

"Of course."

She nodded. There was still fear in her eyes, fear for him. But there was also resolve. "Good," she said. "If you didn't go, you wouldn't be you."

Moved, he touched her face. She came into his arms, but when he didn't move to embrace her, she stiffened. "It's not what you think," he assured her. "My people believe . . . to touch a woman before battle . . ."

She nodded. "Such different customs . . . between your people and mine."

She watched while he finished readying his gear. When he walked out to the stables, carrying his bedroll and saddlebags, she followed a few steps behind, carrying both his rifles. She was silent while she watched him saddle and bridle his horse, then lash his bedroll into place. She handed him the rifles one by one, saying nothing while he thrust them into their saddle scabbards. When he led his horse around to the front of Don Javier's house, she walked by his side.

Don Javier was in the street, watching as Ramon's body

was carried into the house where it would be readied for burial. He immediately noticed Gabe's saddled and bridled mount, the rifles in their saddle scabbards, Gabe's long linen duster, which he seldom wore around town. "You're going, then."

"Yes. Some men need killing."

"Wait awhile. A number of us would like to go with you."

Gabe shook his head. "That's not a good idea. If the men of Los Robles ride into the county seat as a group and shoot up the place, that would ruin any hope you have of getting your land back. Most of you would probably go to jail. Your families would go hungry. It's better if an outsider does it. Someone who is from nowhere."

Don Javier put his hand on Gabe's shoulder and said softly, "To us, my friend, you are no outsider. Which is why we must ride with you."

Gabe was about to protest again, but he noticed that Don Javier held something in his hand. A bundle of papers, slightly stained with blood. "What's that?" he asked.

"Some papers Ramon was about to file. To get the old sheriff reinstated. I guess they killed him before he could actually record them."

Gabe held out his hand. "Let me see."

A few years previously, his Boston lawyer grandfather had tutored him in the law. Gabe was no attorney, but he could decipher legal gibberish. He read through the papers. "They look complete," he told Don Javier.

"What does it matter? . . ."

"A lot. Look . . . if you want to help, the best thing you could do would be to file these papers. As it is now, Harrison's legitimacy as sheriff is cloudy. If these papers are filed, any legitimacy he might currently have will completely evaporate. And if he's not sheriff . . . then he's just another back-shooting assassin. He'll be fair game."

Don Javier's face lit up with comprehension. "Of course. Then we can ride in and—"

"No. I ride in alone."

Don Javier was about to protest again, but he saw the

look of resolve on Gabe's face, suspected that to Gabe, avenging Ramon was something personal. Something to do with honor. And Don Javier had a deep and abiding belief in the importance of honor. "As you wish, my friend," he replied, nodding.

Gabe's departure was delayed while a man was found who was willing to take Ramon's legal papers to the county seat and record them. The man left immediately, mounted on a fast horse, riding hard. The plan was for him to get to the courthouse ahead of Gabe and file the papers with the county clerk as unobtrusively as possible.

An hour later Gabe was ready to ride. The town's entire population gathered in the plaza as he untied his horse from the hitching rack. There were no cheers, no handshakes. "*Vaya con Dios,*" Don Javier said firmly.

Gabe saw Elena standing a few yards away, looking miserable. He walked over to her. She stood awkwardly in front of him, until he took her in his arms, and then she clung to him tightly. A brief, hard kiss, and then they were parted again, but now there was a happy light shining in the girl's eyes. "As I told you the first time you left us," she said fiercely. "Kill the sons of pigs!"

Laughing, Gabe mounted his horse. After one last look at Elena, he rode out, not at all sure he would ever see her again.

Once he'd left the village behind, neither Elena nor anything else in it mattered much. What mattered lay ahead; he was riding out to do a man's work, to right a wrong, to wage war against those who had waged war against the people who had adopted him. As his horse set out on the trail, the heaviness of the life he'd led in the village slid away from Gabe as if it had never existed, had never weighed him down, had never encumbered his soul. He knew then, with certainty, that he would never see Los Robles again.

He rode slowly, he was not in a hurry. There were things to do before he hunted down the men who'd killed Ramon. Of first importance was the cleansing away of all that had tarnished his spirit while he'd been living in the village.

After an hour's lazy riding, he hunted out a small, clear stream. Tying his horse, he dismounted and began stripping off his clothes. Naked, he stepped into the stream and immersed himself in its cool waters. As the current flowed over him, he felt it taking away all the fears and jealousies, all the unworthy thoughts and emotions that had dominated his life in Los Robles. The water also washed away the effects of his last physical contact with Elena. To ride straight into battle after being with a woman was to ask for death. Gabe sent a silent prayer to Wakan Tanka, asking the Great Spirit to cleanse his *ni*, his spirit, to make him once again a pure warrior, a warrior without fear.

Emerging from the stream, Gabe let the warm afternoon air dry his skin. Then he dressed again, taking special care with his weapons, making certain that the holster and knife sheath beneath his right armpit were correctly positioned, and that the holster on his right hip was fastened securely in place so that the leather would not grip his .44 and slow his draw. He removed his rifles from their saddle scabbards, assuring himself that the Winchester's magazine was filled with live rounds and that the Sharps's action was firmly locked in place.

Sure of his weapons, Gabe then unfastened his bedroll. He took off his linen duster and replaced it with the buffalo-hide coat, the one with the image of Wakinyan, the Winged God, painted across the back. And as he put the coat on, as the thunderbird wings settled into place over his shoulders, he felt energy surge through his body. He felt protected, as he had felt protected when, so many years ago, he had first felt those wings settle over him during his vision quest. The real wings, not the painted ones. When Wakinyan had first come to him. When the Winged One had shown him, in images, the direction his life would take. When Wakinyan had shown him the terrible fate of his people.

Fully outfitted, once again a warrior, once again the man called Long Rider, Gabe remounted. The sun was growing lower in the sky. He didn't have much time.

He rode straight to the house where the former sheriff lived. It was about two miles outside town. The sheriff heard him coming, and walked out into the yard to meet him. "Well, hello, son," he said. "You look kind of like a man riding off to war."

"I am, Sheriff."

The other man grimaced. "I'm afraid I'm not the sheriff anymore."

"And I'm sure you are."

Gabe told him then about the papers being filed, how they would invalidate his removal from office. The sheriff smiled. "Time to ride into town, then . . . and get my badge back."

"Not yet," Gabe told him. "There's a little housecleaning to do first."

"Harrison?"

"Among others. You've heard about Ramon being killed?"

The sheriff's eyes narrowed. "Yes. I have."

"That needs to be balanced."

"Mr. Conrad," the sheriff said acerbically. "I'm not in the habit of letting other men do my fighting for me."

"You'd be doing me a big disservice if you rode in now, Sheriff."

The sheriff looked puzzled. "How's that?"

"Those men are mine. I want them. But I need you alive and in office afterward to keep me from hanging. If you ride in now and shoot it out with Harrison, you may lose the office again. Or get killed. Then I swing. But if Harrison's already dead . . ."

"Maybe you're right."

"There is one thing you can do, Sheriff."

The sheriff's eyebrows rose. "And what might that be, Mr. Conrad?"

"Deputize me."

Gabe rode out ten minutes later, with a battered star pinned to the front of his shirt. He was half an hour out of town when he saw the man who'd been sent to the court-house with the papers riding toward him. The two men stopped, stirrup to stirrup. "Did you do it?" Gabe asked.

"Yes. The papers are legally on record. I have a receipt from the clerk."

"Good," was all Gabe said in reply. He nudged his horse into a trot and headed, alone, toward the town. The other man started to call out after him, but changed his mind, and turned his own horse toward Los Robles.

There was only an hour or two of daylight left when Gabe arrived in town. He tied his horse directly in front of the courthouse. Slipping his Winchester from its scabbard, he dismounted. There were not many people on the street, and the few that were there, recognizing Gabe and fully aware of what had happened the day before, hurried to get inside, out of the line of fire.

Gabe walked straight toward the jail, where he had spent too many tense hours inside a cell, wondering if he was going to be hanged. As he walked along the boardwalk he wondered if he might end up hanging, anyhow. Better a bullet than the rope.

He was about fifty yards from the jail when he saw Harrison walk out the front door. Harrison had obviously not spotted him yet. He started walking along the boardwalk as if he did not have a care in the world. Harrison seemed to be walking a little unsteadily. Gabe wondered if Harrison was drunk. If so, it would be his last drunk.

They were only about ten or fifteen yards apart when Harrison saw him. Harrison did an almost comical double take, skidding to a stop, with his mouth hanging open. "Conrad! You . . . here?" he blurted.

"That's right, Harrison. I'm here just to see you. And those Pinkerton killers. You're under arrest, you back-shooting bastard."

"Wh-What?" Harrison spluttered, snorting the words out, along with a lot of spit. "Are you crazy, Conrad?"

Gabe pulled back the edge of his coat, so that Harrison could see the star. "It's all over, Harrison. The old sheriff is back in the saddle again. He deputized me."

"You . . . that's a lie!"

"Too late for that. Either I arrest you or I gun you down right here."

"Arrest me for what?" Harrison demanded.

"The murder of Ramon Garcia."

"It wasn't me. It was those two Pinkertons."

"You were seen shooting Ramon in the back. Around here, they hang back-shooters quicker than they hang horse thieves."

"That's a lie! It was the Pinks." Now Harrison grew crafty. "You don't want to tangle with no Pinks, Conrad. You'd end up with their whole fuckin' agency breathin' down your neck."

Gabe was surprised. He'd expected Harrison to go for his gun the moment he was challenged. He remembered his first meeting with Harrison, when he'd still been John Slaughter's foreman. Earlier, Harrison had been a hard man, a hair-trigger fighter. But perhaps it was that previous meeting itself that had made the change. Perhaps Harrison was now afraid of him. Perhaps he was remembering the way Gabe had shot up his men, the way he'd terrorized an entire town full of hardcase cowhands.

Gabe regretted having shown Harrison his deputy's star. He didn't want to arrest him, he wanted to kill him, avenge Ramon's murder. But it would be stupid to shoot Harrison down in cold blood in broad daylight right in front of the jail. Not that Harrison had hesitated doing exactly that to Ramon. But then, Harrison had better connections than Gabe.

So Gabe started to turn away. "Okay, Harrison. I'll go ask those two Pinkertons. We'll see if their story matches yours."

He completely turned his back on the other man and started to walk away, his Winchester hanging loosely from his right hand, uncocked, unready. And Harrison reacted just as Gabe had expected him to react; he drew on Gabe, ready to shoot him in the back just as he'd shot Ramon. What Harrison was not aware of was that Gabe had set the whole thing up—he could see Harrison's every move reflected in a big plate-glass window across the street.

Even as Harrison was reaching for his pistol, Gabe was reaching for his own, the big Colt .44 that rode on his right

hip, butt forward. When he'd started walking away from
Harrison, his heavy thunderbird coat had billowed out to
the sides, hiding his move, so Harrison was taken completely by surprise. Gabe never even bothered turning all
the way around, just far enough to see Harrison out of the
corner of his eye. Reaching across his body with his left
hand, Gabe pulled the .44 out of the holster, cocked it, and
fired backward between his right arm and his right side.

The bullet bored a neat hole in the buffalo-hide coat, then
continued onward, taking Harrison in the throat. Harrison
flew backward, his arms flying up, his pistol firing harm-
lessly into the air. Finally turning all the way around, Gabe
walked up to Harrison and kicked the pistol out of his hand.

He stood over Harrison, wondering if he should put another bullet in him, but Harrison, choking on his own blood,
eyes crazy with pain and fear, was no longer worth worrying
about. "Once a back-shooter, always a back-shooter,"
Gabe said icily, then turned away. He looked back only
once. Harrison's hands were at his throat. The choking
sounds were louder now; clearly he was no longer able to
breath. Harrison's bootheels drummed wildly against the
boardwalk for another few seconds, then his body arched
in one last great spasm. After that, he lay still.

One down, two to go. Harrison had behaved as if the
two Pinkertons were still in town. If they were, he'd find
them.

It happened the other way around; the Pinkertons found
Gabe. Having heard the shooting, both of them came out
of the saloon and stood on the boardwalk about six feet
apart, watching Gabe as he headed in their direction. From
where they stood they could see Harrison's body, so they
had little doubt that there would be a fight.

Gabe moved up the far side of the street, across from the
saloon, keeping his back close to walls, moving carefully
around windows and doorways. He stopped directly opposite the two Pinkertons. They faced him squarely, their
thumbs hooked in their gun belts. One of them, a big man
wearing a watch chain across his vest, nodded at Gabe. "I

see that you've been busy, mister," he said coolly, jerking his head in Harrison's direction.

"He was first on the list," Gabe replied just as coolly. "You're next . . . for the man you killed yesterday."

"Is that so?" Ned asked casually. There was no more conversation, no more rhetoric—the two Pinkertons were professionals. Sudden action exploded on both sides of the street as the two Pinkertons reached for their guns, and Gabe raised his Winchester and cocked the hammer. Then the details of the fight became lost in a sudden crash of gunfire.

Having the only rifle, Gabe should have held the advantage—except that the Pinkertons had an initial stroke of luck. Ned's first bullet, fired too hastily to hit Gabe, hit the stock of his rifle instead. Gabe felt the shock of the bullet hitting wood, felt his hands tingle, then the Winchester was spinning away, out of reach. He made no attempt to recover the rifle; no telling how badly it was damaged. With empty hands and two deadly gunmen out to kill him, he was not about to spend another second out in the open. Gabe leaped to his right, leaving his feet, rolling when he hit the boardwalk, scrambling toward the mouth of an alley. Bullets tore chunks of wood off the wall right behind where he'd been standing, but he made it into the alley and instantly ducked back out of sight.

"Come on . . . let's get him," Ned shouted to his companion. Together, the two men sprinted toward the alley . . . only to meet Gabe face-to-face. The instant Gabe had ducked out of sight, he'd drawn both his pistols. It took him a moment to squeeze the bent index finger on his right hand around the trigger. Then he headed back toward the street, rebounding like a rubber ball.

Surprise was on his side. The Pinkertons were running hard, their pistols held low. They had to skid to a stop before they could start firing, and by then Gabe was already shooting, firing two handed, both his pistols spitting fire and lead, sending a storm of bullets into the bodies of his opponents.

The two gunmen reeled backward. Ned was able to get off a shot, but the bullet missed Gabe by more than a yard.

Still firing, Gabe walked toward the two staggering gunmen, slamming more bullets into their already-shattered bodies. From the time Gabe charged back out of the alley, the shooting lasted only a few seconds, but the continuous roar of gunfire and the cries of the wounded made it seem much longer. Finally, the two Pinkertons fell in the middle of the street, stunned, mortally wounded, but not yet dead.

Gabe kicked the pistol out of Ned's hand. The other Pinkerton had already lost his. Gabe stood over them, a smoking pistol in each hand. "My only regret," he said, his voice bitter, "is that killing you won't bring back Ramon Garcia. Ramon was far too good a man to exchange for garbage like you."

He raised his pistols, pointing one at the head of each man. He saw the awareness of death in Ned's eyes. "Yeah," Gabe said softly. "In the face. Like Ramon."

His twin .44s roared together. Both Pinkertons were flung full length back onto the ground, their faces bloody pulp. They did not move again. Gabe looked down at what was left of them, then shook his head sadly. "Not worth the trade," he repeated. "Not worth it at all."

CHAPTER FIFTEEN

On the way out of town, Gabe bought a new stock for his Winchester; the old one was badly shattered. No one made the slightest effort to keep him from leaving. He was about a mile from town when he realized that he had no idea where he wanted to go, what direction to take. Common sense said to ride on and keep riding until New Mexico was only a faded memory. But something other than common sense, something inside Gabe, anchored him here. He felt as if a chain had been forged that no longer permitted him freedom of movement.

So he temporized by riding back up into the Sangre de Cristo mountains. Without actually planning it, he headed toward his little valley, the one in which he'd built his sweat lodge. When he arrived, it was as if he had come home. The peace of the valley closed around him like a mother's arms.

Gabe spent the next few days rebuilding his sweat lodge. He put in a new supply of meat, then spent hours cleaning his gear. One of his first acts was to replace his Winchester's broken stock. As before, the valley demanded no speed, no hurrying. He spent an entire day rubbing deer fat into the wood of the new stock, until it glowed. What he had no time for was thinking or planning or ordering his life in any other way. Each day took care of itself. As it should.

However, vigilance was built into Gabe, and he was immediately aware when riders approached his little Eden. Taking both his rifles, he moved to a vantage point that commanded the valley's entrance. As he'd expected, it was Don Javier and several other men from Los Robles. He watched them ride into his campsite. When they did not see him, they looked around uneasily. One of the men flinched when Gabe silently materialized out of the brush right next to his horse. "*Santa Maria!*" the man hissed. "You move like a ghost."

The men dismounted gratefully; they were tired from the long ride. When Don Javier got down from his horse, Gabe saw that the old man was moving as if his bones ached. Apparently he was feeling his age. For too many years he'd borne the burdens of his pueblo. And now . . . with this terrible, ultimate threat of losing their land . . .

"It's not going well," Don Javier told Gabe as the two of them sat together near Gabe's campfire. The other men were sitting nearby, making a large dent in Gabe's meat supply.

"They finally served us with the papers," Don Javier said sadly. "We've hired a lawyer to try to keep us from being physically moved off the land, but it's only a delaying action. If Ramon were still alive . . ."

Gabe was silent for several seconds. "Perhaps," he finally said, "if someone were to talk to the man who has bought your land . . . convince him that keeping it would be . . . dangerous . . ."

Don Javier snorted in exasperation. "Oh, we've thought of that. We've thought of a hundred ways to . . . convince him. But we don't even know who he is! Or if he's only one person! The purchase was made in the name of a corporation. We only know the name of a lawyer in New York. Perhaps there is no one man. Perhaps the land has been bought by a consortium, by faceless investors . . . although I know in my heart that it has to be the Santa Fe Ring. At least some of its members. Ah, how I detest those men."

"So," Gabe said, "there's nothing that can be done. Nothing simple and straightforward."

Don Javier shrugged. "I suppose not. Except stand and fight when they come to take our land. And we'll lose that fight, too."

"Land," Gabe murmured. "In so many places, so many people have died over land, over what should belong equally to all."

"True," Don Javier replied. "And that madness will continue as long as men live by greed."

His face suddenly brightened. "There is one piece of good news. Our old sheriff is back in place. Ramon's idea worked. And he's made your part official, how he deputized you, and how you were acting as an officer of the law when you killed Harrison and those two Pinkertons."

"So . . . I'm off the hook, then."

Don Javier shifted uncomfortably. "Well, with the law, yes. No official charges will be brought against you. But . . . there are other problems."

"The Pinkertons?"

"Yes. They're apart from the law. And some of them, at least the ones in the local office, are . . . upset that you killed two of their own."

"Two of their own?" Gabe asked. "Do you really feel that way? Those two men were hired killers. I can't believe they were working for the Pinkerton Agency other than temporarily. The Pinkertons won't risk trouble to avenge scum like that."

"They will if they're paid," Don Javier replied glumly. "The Pinkertons are in it for the money. First, last, and always the money."

"Ah," Gabe said. "And someone's paying."

"Yes. Apparently someone here in New Mexico. There are Pinkerton posses out looking for you. We had to make very certain that we were not followed here. There must be a dozen men out hunting you, Gabriel. We're all worried. That's why we came here . . . to ask you to come back to Los Robles, where you'll be among people who are willing to protect your life with their own."

"Which is exactly why I will not return. All along, I've only wanted to protect lives, not place a whole town in danger."

"I understand," Don Javier replied, nodding. Gabe thought he could detect just the slightest bit of relief in Don

Javier's manner. He'd had to offer, of course. After what Gabe had done for them, the entire village had to make the offer. Just as Gabe had to refuse.

An hour later, Don Javier and his men were ready to depart. Don Javier swung up into the saddle—once again, rather stiffly—then bent down to shake Gabe's hand. "If I were you," the old man said, "I'd consider riding far from here. If the Pinkertons can't find you, then whoever is paying them locally will tire of it, and the whole thing will be forgotten. You won't have to spend the rest of your life watching your back trail."

"I'll think about it," Gabe replied. "But I ride only when I'm ready to ride."

Don Javier nodded. "You're a man among men, Gabriel. I think the Pinkertons will regret it if they ever do find you. But they are many, and you are only one."

"True. But they haven't found me yet, have they? *Vaya con Dios,* Don Javier. I wish that I could have helped save your land."

"So do I, my friend."

Nodding one last time, Don Javier turned his horse and led his men out of the little valley. Gabe remained standing by the fire until he could no longer see them. And even then he stood, looking toward where the last of them had disappeared. Their visit had jolted him into thinking again. Just why *was* he staying here? Why did he not do as Don Javier had suggested? Leave this land, ride far away, forget its troubles. There was something holding him here, and it was more than pride, more than anger over having men hunting him. Something . . . elusive.

He suddenly became aware of movement off to the right, on a side trail, behind some willows. He froze, intently studying the underbrush, looking for the white flash of a deer's tail or the quick, flickering movements of birds.

No. It was a human. Someone was in the brush, watching him. He could make out part of a horse, and, screened by the willows, the vague shape of a rider.

Gabe's Winchester was a dozen strides away. Could he

get to it before the rider fired? And were there others out
there, too, observing him?

He was tensing his muscles, ready to spring for his rifle,
when the horse and rider came out of the willows onto open
ground. When Gabe saw who it was, all the tension went
out of him. Elena!

She was riding astride, her skirts tucked beneath her
thighs to keep the saddle leather from galling her flesh. She
rode her horse slowly into the middle of the campsite. So
far she had not said a word. Her face was solemn, set in a
silent question, which Gabe interpreted as, "Are you glad
that I'm here?" But when she finally spoke, she said simply,
"I followed the others. I knew they were coming to see
you."

Gabe nodded. "But if you were able to follow, others
might have followed, too."

She shook her head. "No one did. I kept checking my
back trail."

"You could have been fooled," Gabe insisted. "Look
how you fooled Don Javier and his men."

Elena slowly shook her head again. "I fooled no one.
Or it might be better to say we were all fooling one another.
They knew I would come. The whole village knew it. They
knew I would try to find you, and they let me, without
exactly saying that I could. It's a way we Spanish have of
doing that which must be done, but which our customs say
should not be done."

Gabe nodded solemnly. "I approve. It's an intelligent
way to behave."

By now, both were aware that each was playing a very
pleasant game with the other. Knowing, they stretched it
out, both speaking formally, each of them holding in check
the emotions rioting inside their brains. And then, as if on
cue, they both burst out laughing. "Oh, Gabriel," Elena
said, sliding down from her horse. "How happy I am to see
you."

As Gabe took Elena into his arms, he was aware that she
had somehow subtly changed. The little girl was gone. A
woman now stood in her place. A woman who was totally

aware of the difficulties of their situation. A woman who was able to accept those limitations, who was ready to enjoy what little of Gabe she could have, without asking for that which could not be.

They moved with decorum. First they took care of Elena's horse, staking it out close to Gabe's. There was no frantic clutching of bodies. Elena ate, with neither she nor Gabe saying much. After they'd eaten, Elena stretched, then smiled. "I feel so dirty from the ride. I'm going to take a bath."

Gabe smiled back. "I'll take one with you."

They went down to the stream. Gabe watched as Elena slowly undressed. He watched the way her muscles moved as she carefully placed her clothing on a flat rock. He watched the play of light and shadow on her skin, saw how naturally she moved, as if being naked out of doors was the most natural thing in the world. As, of course, it was.

In this mountain setting, with Elena's body framed by trees and willows, with the water running slowly behind her, the mood of sensuality was heightened. When Elena finally stepped into the water, Gabe quickly undressed and followed.

They made love in the water, moving slowly at first, with many experimental strokings, as if they were touching one another for the first time, which, in a sense, they were—two people different from when they had last touched; Gabe, a free man again, Elena, a woman, not a girl.

They spent three days together. They seldom dressed; clothing did not seem necessary. Gabe filled his mind with images of Elena's naked body moving easily, naturally, through the cottonwoods and alders. As easily as one of the spirit women his people used to talk about, a special spirit of this magic place. He packed images of her into his mind, suspecting that soon enough those images would be all he had left of his time with Elena.

As they lay in his bedroll at night after making love, warm and sticky with one another, she told him why it was now possible for her to come to him with the full knowledge of the village, and then return without losing anyone's respect. "The people realize that because of all this trouble we cannot just simply marry. That you must be . . . free to move. Because of that, in their hearts they consider us already married. So I don't incur any shame."

What she did not say was that she hoped he would make her pregnant. But without hearing the words, he knew, and he worked hard to give her a child. Pleasant work.

Eventually their idyll had to end. "I've been careless, staying here in camp too long," he told her. "I have to ride out and see what . . . the people who are hunting me are doing."

He saw the instant of alarm in her eyes. He expected her to say, "Be careful." Indeed, she almost said it, but she caught herself. This was the new Elena, the warrior's woman. "I'll come back in a few days," she said. "I'll bring news, I'll try to find out all I can."

They rode out together the morning of the fourth day. They rode stirrup to stirrup, Gabe aware of how well Elena sat her horse. He'd never noticed before, but now he was noticing many new things about this girl who had grown before his eyes into a woman. He was finally fully aware of just what it was that bound him so closely to this New Mexican land.

They were halfway down the mountain when they spotted the Pinkerton posse. And were spotted in return. The Pinkertons were about a mile away; a deep gorge separated the two groups. Gabe took out his binoculars and studied the Pinkertons. He picked out their leader, who was looking back at him through another pair of binoculars.

For the moment, with that deep gorge lying in the way, the Pinkertons were in no position to start an immediate pursuit. "We'll ride together for a while," Gabe said to Elena. "Then split up later."

They rode up a slope, in plain view, but once on the other side, it was time for Elena to head back for Los Robles. "I'll lose them," Gabe said. "Then go back to my camp. After I've led them in another direction."

His words were an unspoken invitation for Elena to come

back to his camp within the few days she'd mentioned earlier. Both knew how dangerous that might be—for both of them. Both knew that she would return anyhow, and that Gabe would be there waiting for her.

There were no emotional good-byes; they were both beyond the need for that. They touched hands, then Elena turned her horse. "*Hasta luego*," she called softly back over her shoulder. "Until later."

CHAPTER SIXTEEN

Gabe continued riding along the reverse side of the slope, still out of view of the Pinkertons below, so that Elena would have a chance to get far away before it was noticed that he was now riding alone. Finally, he crested the ridge that hid him from the Pinkertons. The deep gorge still lay between Gabe and the posse, but apparently anticipating that their quarry would continue uphill, the Pinkertons had made considerable distance along their own side of the gorge.

Once again, hunted and hunter stopped to appraise the opposition. Gabe studied the posse leader through his binoculars. He was too far away for Gabe to make out his features—particularly since the other man spent most of the time with binoculars covering the upper part of his face, studying Gabe in return—but Gabe could see that he was a big man.

Gabe turned his horse and started up the slope again. He'd been in these mountains long enough to know the terrain well, and as he rode, he planned his strategy. A few miles ahead, the gorge rose almost to ridge level; up there, the Pinkertons would have little trouble getting around behind him. But they'd have to ride through much rougher country, so Gabe should be able to gain some ground.

He rode steadily, without pushing his horse too hard; he'd need the animal in good condition. He made sure that the posse had ample opportunity to catch glimpses of him as he rode; he wanted them to continue following him, and not Elena.

He reached the crossover point about a mile ahead of the Pinkertons. Here they would be able to ride over to his side of what was left of the gorge. Instead, Gabe crossed over first, to their side, still well ahead of the posse, making certain once again that they saw him.

Riding out of sight, he dismounted. Then, taking the Sharps, he crawled to a point where he could watch his back trail without being seen. He saw the posse reach the point where he'd crossed over. Instead of coming straight after him, they stopped for a conference. Through his glasses Gabe could see the leader talking to the others. One man nodded, then pulled his horse to the right, heading toward the far side of the gorge.

The man was undoubtedly going after Elena. Cursing the posse leader's resourcefulness, Gabe quickly cocked the Sharps, then sighted on the rider. It would be a long shot, but not an impossible one. Gabe carefully squeezed the trigger.

`Ka-blamm!`

It was such a long shot that the big white cloud of smoke that billowed from the Sharps's muzzle had cleared by the time Gabe saw the bullet strike. Damn! He'd fired short!

Gabe reloaded, then raised the bar sight a little higher, but by now, knowing that he was under fire, the rider had picked up his pace and was zigzagging his horse from side to side in an attempt to make the next shot more difficult for Gabe.

But Gabe did not fire immediately. Hitting a zigzagging target at this range would be more a matter of luck than of skill. But Gabe had already noticed that the trail the rider was on narrowed about a hundred yards ahead of where he was now. Narrowed and turned. The rider would have to nearly stop his mount when he came to the turn.

Gabe sighted in on the turn, waiting. He would have to fire at the bottleneck a second or two before the rider reached it. He would have to hope that bullet and rider arrived at the same spot at the same instant. Nothing to do but wait. Only another few yards, now . . .

The rifle roared again. For a couple of seconds it seemed as if nothing had happened, although Gabe was almost certain that he could see the huge bullet arcing toward the turn. Then the rider rode into the bottleneck, and as Gabe had expected, he was forced to slow almost to a stop so that he could maneuver his horse around a huge rock.

Suddenly the horse went down hard, like a poleaxed steer. The rider fell off the far side, banging into the rock. Bullet and target had met.

Some of the posse members were now firing back up at Gabe, but their lighter-caliber Winchesters could not hope to reach him at this distance. Gabe reloaded the Sharps, then laid it aside and picked up his binoculars again. First, the rider. For a moment the fallen man lay still, then, realizing that he was out in the open, he scrambled around behind the big rock.

Back to the posse. Gabe saw the posse leader sitting his horse motionlessly, staring up in his direction. Gabe swapped glasses for rifle again, and laid a shot down close to the posse. Seeing what had happened to the rider who'd gone after Elena, the posse members immediately scattered, searching for cover.

Gabe waited. After a few minutes he saw men edging their horses back toward the trail. Gabe fired again, this time kicking up dirt under the belly of a man's horse. The horse, startled, began to buck, nearly throwing its rider.

The possemen raced back toward cover. Gabe smiled. They were learning. What they did not know was that he had no intention of killing any of them—unless they forced him to. There was no point in stirring up the Pinkerton Agency any more than he already had. Don Javier had said that someone local must be paying the Pinks. Good. He'd lead the Pinks a merry chase, run up the expenses, and hope whoever was paying the bill got tired of the expense and called off his dogs.

About five minutes later, Gabe quietly slipped away, back toward his horse. It would probably be half an hour before the Pinkertons knew that he was gone. He'd use the time to build up a safe lead. But he would be careful not to lose them completely. Not yet.

For the next few hours, Gabe taunted the posse, always keeping well ahead, but letting them catch occasional glimpses of him. From time to time he stopped to study his pursuers through his binoculars. Their leader impressed him. A tenacious man, and one with considerable skill in following a trail.

An hour before dark, Gabe knew that it was time to end the chase. So far he'd been careful to leave a trail that indicated he was trying to hide his tracks, but nevertheless, a trail that was not impossible to follow.

Now he would hide his trail completely. It was not too difficult; all day long he'd been leading the posse toward an area of his own choosing. Here the ground became very hard and was cut by numerous small streams. An easy place to lose the posse. True, in daylight a good tracker might still be able to follow, but there was not much daylight left. Night was coming on fast.

Using every trick he knew, Gabe effectively blotted out his own trail. He was about half a mile away, hidden high on a crag, when the posse came to the point where he had started his evasive maneuvers. Gabe had to admire the way their leader managed to pick up his spoor a couple of times, but by now it was almost dark. Further tracking would be next to impossible.

As Gabe had expected, the posse made camp for the night. He'd half hoped they'd just ride away, back toward the valleys and the towns below. But they did not. Obviously, they intended tracking him again in the morning. They were set for a long chase.

Instead of using the night to gain more distance, Gabe set up his own well-hidden camp much closer to the posse than any of them imagined. Or so he hoped. Meanwhile, he watched. As most white men were prone to do, the Pinkertons made far too large a fire. How easy it would be to move close to the camp and pick off a few posse members by the light of their own fire.

But he still did not want to kill. So while he watched, Gabe busied his hands with lengths of a piece of light rope that he had cut up. Patiently, he twisted and knotted.

Eventually the fire below burned low. There had been a small crescent moon, but it was now close to setting. Judging that the time was finally right, Gabe left his camp on foot, carrying the things he'd made. He was able to walk quickly at first; within ten minutes he was only a hundred yards from the posse's camp.

Now he must be more cautious. His moccasins helped. He'd often wondered how white men could stand their tight, clumsy boots. He moved over the ground silently until he was only about twenty yards from the camp, then he halted in a patch of brush.

Everyone inside the camp seemed to be sleeping. He could hear several of them snoring. A guard had been posted about forty yards outside the campsite on a small knoll. But the guard's attention was focused outward, away from camp. Good. Gabe intended to work from within the camp.

Lying on his belly, Gabe slowly worked his way inward, using every patch of grass, every shrub, to conceal his movements. Crawling the last ten yards took over half an hour. Several times, men turned over in their sleep or abruptly stopped snoring. Each time, Gabe froze and lay unmoving. But none of the men completely awoke.

Gabe could see the guard nodding off from time to time. Each time he did, the guard would jerk awake with a perceptible start, then continue staring out into the darkness, away from the unexpected danger behind him, within the camp.

Gabe spent half an hour slowly crawling from man to man, leaving a gift behind for the leader and several others. As he paused by the posse's leader, Gabe spent a few minutes studying his sleeping face. It was a strong face. A different kind of face from what he'd expected. He saw in it none of the cold cruelty he'd noticed on the faces of the two Pinkertons he'd killed in town. This must be one of the agency's professionals. The man had a face Gabe could respect. Nevertheless, he left his gift.

Now it was time for the final act, perhaps the most dangerous part of what he intended to do. This time there would be a much greater chance of noise. Noise which might bring the sleeping men awake, which would probably prove fatal for Gabe. So that he could move more quietly, he had left his weapons behind in his own camp. He was unarmed.

Using the same care that had gotten him into the camp, Gabe crawled toward the sentry. Within ten minutes he was directly behind the man. But how to deal with him?

Then Gabe got a break. The sentry abruptly stood up. Gabe, thinking that he must have been heard, froze in place, waiting for the sentry's challenge. But none came. Instead, the man stomped his feet a few times to restore circulation to cramped muscles, then walked over toward a bush and began to unbutton his fly.

He'd left his rifle behind. Gabe reached for it. He crouched, muscles tensed, ready to spring on the guard from behind and knock him out. But he hesitated. This entire operation would turn out much more effectively if he left the guard unmolested.

So he stole away quietly, the slight sound of his movements covered by the splash of the steady stream the guard was sending down against the ground.

The posse's leader had made an uncharacteristic error. The horses had been tied about twenty yards from the camp, on the far side from where the guard had been posted. No Indian, living in a world where horse stealing was the preferred sport, would have made that mistake.

Reaching the horses, Gabe was careful to make each of his moves non-threatening; he did not want to spook what he knew were easily spooked animals. Moving among the horses slowly, he carefully untied them. It was easy; they were all attached to one central line. Taking the line in his right hand, he quickly vaulted up onto the back of a big gelding, an animal that the others would probably follow. He nudged the horse into a walk.

There was a certain amount of snorting and stamping among the horses. Any moment Gabe expected a challenge to be shouted after him. But nothing happened. Gabe was able to ride away quietly, with all the other horses following on the lead rope. Perhaps the guard had fallen asleep again.

Gabe took the horses to a small box canyon near where he was camped. Tying them securely, he walked back to camp, where he made himself comfortable in a place where he could observe the men below. Now there was nothing to do but wait.

It grew light long before the sun came up; the sheer rise of mountains to the east delayed the sunrise. One of the posse members, aware of a near-bursting bladder, groaned a couple of times, then decided to get up and do something about it. Maybe, if he was quiet, Rafe wouldn't wake up, and he could get some more shut-eye.

It wasn't until the man was sitting up, ready to rub sleep from his eyes, that he became aware of something dragging lightly at his right arm. Annoyed, he looked down, uncomprehending at first, then he stiffened. A crudely made hangman's noose was looped over his arm. "Jesus," he grunted, wondering which of his fellow posse members had played the trick.

It was not until he glanced around the camp and noticed similar nooses draped over, or next to, several other posse members that he realized that it was not a trick aimed at him alone. "Rafe!" he bellowed.

His shout awakened the entire camp. Rafe, the posse leader, came awake more quickly than most of the rest. The man who'd shouted was holding up his noose. Rafe quickly realized that it was not the only one, that a noose had been laid over his bedroll, not far from his throat.

Rafe was out of his bedroll and on his feet in one smooth movement. "Hank!" he shouted.

The guard, stiff and sleepy from his long vigil, had already been alerted by the commotion in the camp. He came stumbling toward Rafe, of whom he was mortally afraid.

"You son of a bitch," Rafe snarled. "You fell asleep!"

"No I didn't, Rafe. So help me God."

"Then how did that bastard get into our camp?" Rafe demanded, holding up his noose.

"Gawd . . . I dunno."

Nor did the other men. "Like a fuckin' ghost," one of them murmured.

"Jesus. He coulda cut the throat of ever' last livin' one of us," another said.

Thinking of their quarry, slipping into their camp at night, lying next to them as they slept, maybe with a big knife in his hand, gave each of them the chills. "Thank God he's got a sense o' humor," one man said gratefully.

Gabe's trick had shaken Rafe, too, but he refused to show it. "If that sneaky son of a bitch spent the night here, that means he's close. So let's break camp, mount up, and get on his trail."

Which was when they discovered that their horses were missing. Realizing the extent of the disaster, Rafe felt his face turning a fiery brick red. The others shrank away; they'd had opportunities to learn to fear Rafe's present mood.

But the expected outburst did not materialize. Instead, the other men watched Rafe grow icy cold. "I'm going to get that bastard if it's the last thing I do," he murmured, more to himself than to the others.

They watched him pace for a while. Finally, his face lit up. "The girl!" he burst out.

"Uh . . . what girl?" one of the men asked.

"The one that was riding with Conrad, you idiot. Remember how he shot Charlie's horse out from under him when I sent Charlie to look for her trail? She's the key. She's gotta be. We'll have to find out who the hell she is."

It did not take long for the Pinkertons, with their local resources, to find out about Gabe and Elena. Their romance was, by now, a famous local story. Watchers were posted not far away from Los Robles. Several days later, when Elena left the village to seek out Gabe, she had no idea at all that she was being watched through powerful binoculars.

CHAPTER SEVENTEEN

Gabe was growing restless. He'd been cooped up in his little valley too damned long. With men out looking for him, staying in one place was not good. But if he didn't remain in the valley, how would Elena be able to find him?

He'd ridden out twice, and found no signs of the Pinkerton posse. Perhaps they'd been scared off for good. He smiled as he remembered the consternation in the Pinkerton camp when they'd found the nooses.

This particular morning, Gabe was especially nervous. He promised himself that if Elena did not show up by nightfall, he'd leave first thing in the morning. To pass the time, he saddled his horse, stuffed his rifles into their saddle scabbards, and rode toward the upper end of the valley, where it narrowed. Here the path was nothing but a game trail, a slight break in the undergrowth, so narrow that only one horse at a time could pass.

After checking the arrangements he had made, Gabe rode back toward camp. He stopped two hundred yards short. There was something wrong; he could sense it. He'd become intensely sensitive to every aspect, every nuance of the valley. He knew its every trail, he knew a good many of the individual animals that lived here.

The birds were silent, that was it. Too silent . . . as if something had frightened them. They were used to him, they wouldn't fall silent on his account.

Then a deer came crashing out of a thicket at the lower end of the canyon. It saw Gabe, but did not run back toward the thicket. Instead, it came on toward him in a leaping, zigzagging run, then angled off to one side.

Gabe pulled out his Winchester and guided his horse into a small grove of trees, where he sat, motionless, waiting, blending in with the landscape.

There was movement in a thicket farther down the valley. A moment later Elena rode out into the open. Gabe, still hidden, watched her approach. How gracefully she sat her horse. It made him feel good just to see her riding toward him.

She rode right into the center of his camp. She did not dismount, but sat her horse, looking around, no doubt wondering where he was. Gabe remained hidden, watching the thicket from which she'd appeared. Only when he was certain that there was no one else concealed there did he finally ride out into the open.

Elena saw him when he was about a hundred yards away. He could see the glad smile that broke over her face, and then she was riding toward him, kicking her horse into a run. He nudged his own mount into a canter. They met just outside the camp and leaned toward one another for a kiss. "I was wondering if you were really going to show up," Gabe said.

She gave a helpless little shrug. "After we saw those men the last time I was here, I thought I should wait awhile. But I couldn't wait any longer. So . . . here I am."

They rode into the campsite side by side, neither of them feeling the need to say much. Gabe felt easy with Elena and suspected she felt the same with him. It was almost as if they were beginning to experience things together, as one person, a much more satisfying relationship than the one they'd had in Los Robles, with all its games and subterfuges.

They dismounted and hitched their horses to some shrubbery. "Are you hungry?" Gabe asked.

"Dying of hunger."

Gabe went over to his drying rack and removed a couple of strips of venison. He handed one to Elena. She bit off a chunk. "Tough," she said, grimacing.

"That's what life is like out here."

She laid the piece of meat down on a rock. "I think I can change that. I brought a pot and some potatoes and carrots. We can cook a stew."

"That'd be good."

Elena started toward her horse; Gabe could see the pot lashed behind the saddle. Then something beyond Elena's horse, at the far end of the valley, attracted his attention. He saw several crows flap heavily into the air from the top of a tree. He recognized their raucous cries as an alarm call.

Suddenly the very air felt heavy with menace. He saw something move near where the crows had been. "Elena!" he said sharply. "Look out!"

They rode out of the thickets, a dozen armed men. They were heading straight for the camp, and all had guns in their hands. Elena had looked up when Gabe called to her. When she saw the men, she paled. "*¡Madre de Dios!*" she murmured.

"Quick!" Gabe said, his voice low but intense. "Get behind the rocks."

The campsite was partially ringed by boulders, some of them higher than a man. Gabe grabbed the reins of both horses and led the animals behind the boulders. As soon as he and Elena were behind cover, he slipped his Winchester from its saddle scabbard and took up a position where he could cover the men below.

He recognized one of them, the big man, the leader, the one that the others had called Rafe. And Rafe had recognized him. "Come on, boys," Rafe called out. "Let's rush 'em."

The Pinkertons spurred their horses into a run. They were perhaps three hundred yards away. "Oh my God, I must have led them here," Elena said, her voice anguished.

"Perhaps, perhaps not," Gabe replied, although he was certain that she was right. "Don't waste time feeling bad. We're going to have to work hard to get out of here in one piece."

The Pinkertons were only two hundred yards away when Gabe opened fire. The posse had to be slowed down, so Gabe was shooting for volume of fire rather than for accuracy. Most of his shots missed, but one of his bullets plucked an attacker from the saddle. Another clutched at an arm that had been grazed by a bullet. And a horse went down.

Gabe was aware of the sharp crack of a rifle being fired close to his left. He turned. Elena was shooting, too; she'd come armed. He saw a hat fly off the head of one of the posse members. For a split second Gabe held his fire, mesmerized by the look of intense concentration on Elena's face. He felt proud of her; she was the right kind of woman to ride alongside a warrior.

The posse members, suffering under a punishing fire directed at them from behind cover, did the natural thing— they raced for the cover of the trees and brush.

"This is our chance," Gabe told Elena. "While they're disorganized, we'll make a run for it."

"Your poor camp, they'll wreck it," Elena said, remembering the joy she'd experienced here.

"Better they get the camp than get us."

He realized how lucky they were that the horses had been saddled and close at hand when the attack came. If the posse had chosen half an hour later to make their move, they would probably have found Gabe and Elena lying naked on top of Gabe's bedroll. The thought had been in his mind; he'd been entranced by Elena's swaying hips when she'd walked toward her horse to fetch the cooking pot.

Time to ride! Gabe took a moment to watch how smoothly his woman vaulted into the saddle. Then they were on their way, riding hell for leather toward the upper valley and that narrow path. Gabe heard the man called Rafe shout something, followed a moment later by other loud cries and the thunder of hooves as the posse tore after them.

Guns roared. Gabe could hear the nasty wicker of bullets passing close by. He turned in the saddle and fired two shots from his Winchester. He saw Elena about to do the same, but he shouted at her, "Don't stop! Ride! Ride like hell!"

The ground he and Elena were racing over was level; this was a fairly open part of the valley. Ahead, where the valley narrowed, the ground cover grew thicker. They'd be forced to slow, and the Pinkertons would gain on them. But once they reached cover, they'd have a better chance. He could already make out the place where the trail narrowed, the point where it would pass only one horse at a time. Just a little farther now.

The volume of fire from behind was not only greater, but it was closer. The posse was gaining! As Gabe and Elena rode into the brush and woods, bullets were clipping twigs from around them. Just a few more strides, then they'd be on that narrow trail, just before the point where it took a sharp bend to the right. Once around that bend, they'd be out of sight . . . and maybe home free. Gabe suspected that the posse members would hesitate before charging blindly into such a narrow place.

But they did not get away quite free. Just as they reached the place where the trail bent to the right, he heard a meaty smack, followed by a sharp cry from Elena.

He turned. She was slumped forward in her saddle, head down, obviously struggling for air. "Are you hit?" he shouted.

Elena's head came up. "I . . . I'm all right," she replied. Her voice was strong, so he believed her. "You ride ahead," he said. They could no longer ride abreast; the trail was growing very narrow.

It was only when she got ahead of him that he could see the blood about halfway up her back, somewhat to the right of center; a lot of blood, and in a dangerous place. He immediately knew that Elena had been wounded badly. Yet she was riding fairly well. There was not much he could do about it, anyhow—he could not even ride up alongside her.

What was left of the little valley began to narrow around them. Nearly sheer walls rose on either side. Finally they reached the point he'd been looking for. Here, on the slopes above them, the ground was very unstable. Gabe, always looking for safe exits, had spent the better part of a day shoring up the unstable rocks and earth above the trail with branches and bushes. Now, as he and Elena rode past, he tugged at a trailing piece of limb that he'd wedged in with the other limbs and debris. Almost immediately rocks and dirt began to fall. He spurred his horse forward, narrowly missing being buried by an avalanche of rock and dirt. When he looked back, a cloud of dust hung above a mound of rock ten feet deep that stretched from wall to wall of the chasm through which they had just passed.

They were safe now; it would take the Pinkertons at least two hours to clear away the debris. Two hundred yards ahead the trail opened out again. Easy riding. "Just a little farther," Gabe called to Elena.

As soon as there was room, he rode up alongside her. He saw immediately that she was in a very bad condition. She was reeling in the saddle, her face colored an ashen gray. Gabe reached over and steadied her. "There's water ahead. When we reach it, we can do something about your wound."

By the time they reached the water, a deep pool in a small stream, Elena had grown so weak that she would have fallen from her horse if Gabe hadn't been holding her up. He slid off the wrong side of his own horse, then eased her down onto the ground. Her head was hanging with a terrible, slack looseness, and for a moment he thought that she was not breathing. "Elena!" he cried.

But as he lay her down on the grass next to the little pool, her eyes opened. She did not seem to see him for a moment, then she focused on his face. "Gabriel," she murmured.

"*Shhhhh* . . . be quiet. Save your strength. You're going to be all right."

Privately, he was not so sure. He rolled her over partway, so that he could pull up the back of her blouse. Wiping away the blood, he saw the bullet wound, a blue puckered hole. Almost immediately, more blood pumped out of the wound. He heard Elena began to choke. Tearing off a piece of her blouse, he wadded it up and packed it against the bullet hole, then lay her down on top of it, hoping that would stop the bleeding.

Her eyes found his face again. "It . . . it doesn't hurt much," she managed to say. "I . . . I thought . . ."

How weak her voice was. Anguish flooded through Gabe. "Elena . . . I'm so sorry . . ."

She smiled. "Don't be sorry, Gabriel. To have been with you even for a little while . . ."

"Don't talk like that! I'll go back and get them to help you. The Pinkertons . . ."

"Gabriel . . . Don't be sad . . ."

Her voice had grown even fainter; Gabe had to lean close to hear what she said. Her eyes were still on his face. He saw the warmth in them, the love. "Elena . . . ," he murmured.

She seemed unaware of his words. "So . . . beautiful . . . ," she whispered in a voice so low he could barely hear at all. She seemed to be looking right through him. A moment later he became aware that while her eyes were still open, they were no longer seeing him. They were no longer seeing anything.

Softly, gently, Gabe closed Elena's sightless eyes. He knelt for a moment, staring down at her dead body, hardly able to comprehend what had happened. She had only just begun to live!

Gabe was suddenly on his feet. He did not know how he got there. He simply stood up, body rigid, hands clenched into fists, eyes wild, but not nearly as wild as the terrible cry that burst from his throat. A cry full of grief. A cry that demanded vengeance.

A quarter of a mile away, behind the rockfall that blocked the trail, the possemen heard that cry. "Jesus!" one man said, awed. "What the hell was that?"

"I dunno," Rafe replied. But as the sound of Gabe's cry faded away, echoing and re-echoing among the hills, Rafe felt a cold chill run up and down his spine. So did every man there.

CHAPTER EIGHTEEN

In his wandering through the mountains, Gabe had discovered a place he loved, a place of particular beauty. It was a small glade set in the midst of a cottonwood grove about five miles from his camp. He took Elena's body there, lashed across the back of her horse. When he reached the glade, he gently took the body down and laid it on a bed of leaves. He stood for a while, immobile, looking down at her lovely face, remembering . . .

He did not know how long he stood there, but he finally broke free of his recollections and set to work. Using his heavy sheath knife, he cut several medium-sized branches, which he used to build a platform. He lashed the platform into place between the trunks of four cottonwood trees, about seven feet above the ground. The entire structure took less than an hour to build. When it was finished, he walked back to where Elena lay. She looked quite peaceful.

The time for looking was over. The time for action was near. He took the girl's blankets from her horse and wrapped them around her body, covering her completely, even her face. Then he lifted her up onto the platform. He placed Elena's rifle and her saddle and bridle next to her body. She had been a warrior's companion, she had fought like a Lakota woman, and she would lie in death like a Lakota woman, above the ground, facing the sky, with the sun and moon shining down on her, with the wind free to touch her body. Eventually the birds would take her flesh, returning her body to the world from which it had been formed. Most

importantly, she would not be abandoned to rot in a wet,
dark hole in the ground.

Gabe drew his knife, ready to slash his arms and chest,
as he had done when his mother and his wife had been
killed. A time when he had mourned. But he stopped himself. Loss of blood would weaken him, and he would need
a great deal of strength for what he had to do. He put the
knife away.

He looked one last time at the unmoving, shrouded figure
that lay above him. He placed his right hand on Elena's
body. "You will not be the only one to die today," he
promised. "Others will join you."

Now it was time to fulfill that promise. He took everything
off his horse that was not needed; his bedroll, the saddlebags, anything that would slow the animal in a fight. He
then stripped himself, taking off his pants and shirt. He put
on a breechclout. No need to mimic the white man's way
today. Naked, he would be able to move much more freely
while he fought.

Gabe started a small fire. When it had burned down, he
used some of the charcoal to paint patterns on his face,
arms, and chest. In his saddlebags, inside a small deerskin
pouch, he had other pigments: red ocher and berry juices.
He used them to add to the patterns until he felt that he was
adequately painted for war. He tied his hair behind his head
so that it would not get in his eyes while he fought.

The last thing he did before he left the glade was to turn
Elena's horse loose. With luck it would return to Los Robles. The riderless horse would let the people of the village
know that Elena would not be returning. Finally, Gabe rode
out of the valley alone, a Lakota warrior ready for the
warpath.

His quarry was not difficult to find. Rafe, a tenacious
man, had quickly realized that getting past the deadfall of
rock that Gabe had engineered inside the gorge would waste
too much time. He ordered his men back down the valley.
"We'll break up in groups of three and fan out through the
mountains. It's difficult terrain. There are only a few directions the son of a bitch can head and still stay on a horse.

The first man to spot him will fire a couple of shots, and the rest of us will head that way."

"What's to keep him from ridin' right on out o' here?" one of the men asked.

"You saw the blood. We hit one of 'em hard. They'll probably have to hole up somewhere."

"It was the girl got hit."

"Yeah. I know. Bad luck. I don't like shootin' women. But that'll be even more likely to slow Conrad down. He obviously thought a lot of that girl."

"That's hard thinkin', Rafe."

Rafe shrugged. "It's a hard world."

They fanned out in four groups. Rafe had started with a dozen men, including himself. One man had been killed when they'd first rushed Gabe. Another had been unhorsed. So three of the groups had three men apiece, including Rafe's group. Two men, riding double, made up the fourth. Everyone knew they'd lag far behind, but Rafe would rather have them out looking for Conrad than back in camp, sitting on their asses.

One of the groups was led by a man named Jed. He took his two men high up into the mountains. After a couple of hours of seeing nothing but an occasional deer, all three Pinkertons were less than enthusiastic. Eventually they found themselves in a small, inviting valley. "Gawd, Jed," one of the men groused. "We oughta get down off these here nags for a spell. My ass feels like somebody took a meat ax to it."

"If Rafe figures we're goofin' off, he'll take a meat ax to your head," Jed groused back.

"Well, how the hell will he know? . . ."

The man abruptly shut up. A horseman was riding out of a grove of trees about two hundred yards away. "Jesus!" the man who'd been complaining burst out. "An Injun!"

Jed nodded. "Looks like a Sioux. Didn't know there was any down this way."

"He sure as hell don't look friendly. He's all painted up like he's out shoppin' for scalps. An' he's holdin' on to a rifle."

"Hope there ain't no more of 'em hidin' back in those trees."

The warrior surprised them all by calling out in perfect English, "Do you find this a good day to die, woman killers?"

Jed leaned forward in his saddle, squinting. "Jesus! I think that's the man we're after!"

"Naw . . . it couldn't be!"

There was no more time for them to discuss the matter. Gabe let out a loud whoop and kicked his horse into a run straight toward them. The ground between Gabe and the three Pinkertons was fairly flat and open, dotted here and there by clumps of underbrush and stunted trees. He'd ridden perhaps fifty yards before the Pinkertons were able to recover from their surprise. "Git him, boys . . . 'fore he gets us!" Jed shouted, tugging his Winchester free of its saddle scabbard.

Those were Jed's last words. About a hundred and twenty yards away, a puff of white smoke blossomed from the muzzle of Gabe's rifle. The bullet drilled a hole right through the center of Jed's chest.

The other two men were firing now. Gabe pulled his horse to the left, toward a clump of brush. The men saw him disappear behind the brush, apparently unhit by the half dozen bullets they'd sent his way.

The two Pinkertons stopped to catch their breath, then Gabe abruptly appeared on the opposite side of the brush, swerving back toward them. The Pinkertons fired again, but Gabe was riding low, hanging off the far side of his horse, offering an almost impossible target. Resting his rifle on his horse's withers, Gabe fired a second time, and another man fell.

The lone survivor, sensing that one-to-one odds against the painted killer racing toward him were not at all favorable, pulled his horse around and tried to ride away. But Gabe's horse was bigger and faster, and Gabe quickly ran the Pinkerton down. The Pinkerton turned and fired, but missed. Half out of his mind with fear, he threw his rifle away, wondering why he was still alive. His pursuer could have shot him in the back easily.

Full of contempt and anger, Gabe rode alongside the fleeing man, then knocked him from the saddle with the barrel of his Winchester. The Pinkerton hit hard, rolled, then lay still on the ground, dazed. Gabe leaped down from his horse and stood over the man. Looking up into Gabe's painted face, into those cold gray eyes, the Pinkerton felt overwhelming fear. "Please, mister . . . don't kill me," he whined. "I'm just doin' a job."

Gabe's insides churned. To a Lakota warrior, and he was all Lakota at the moment, nothing was more contemptible than cowardice. This whining dog did not deserve to live. "For Elena," he snarled, and shot the man through the head.

Gabe was startled by the sound of distant shots. The three other groups of Pinkertons had heard the firing, and each group had immediately fired several shots in return to indicate that they were on their way. Gabe was grateful for those answering shots. How stupid of his enemies, how convenient for him. Now he knew their approximate positions. They had obviously split up into small groups.

He could use that knowledge. By now, Gabe's blood had cooled a little. He'd been acting recklessly. True, he'd already killed three of Elena's killers, but he could just as easily have been killed himself. It was time to stop showing off, time to start using his head. No more charging one against three. He smiled. It was time to act like a sneaky Indian.

One group of shots had sounded much closer than the others. Judging from their direction, the men in that group would have to ride up a narrow, heavily wooded trail to reach the scene where the first three men had been killed. Gabe knew that he could reach that trail well before the Pinkertons.

The three men in this second group were overconfident, worried that all that firing ahead meant that somebody else had nailed the man they were after. They'd wanted their own chance at him. In their overconfidence, they rode care-

lessly, strung out along the trail, with one man lagging
behind by more than twenty yards.

Gabe, sitting on a limb fifteen feet above the trail, well
hidden in thick foliage, let the first two ride by underneath.
As the third man passed below, he dropped the noose he'd
been holding. It settled around the man's neck. The velocity
of the man's horse, plus a quick upward tug from Gabe,
fastened the noose firmly in place. The other end of the
rope had been tied to a strong branch, and when the man
reached the end of the slack, he was pulled right out of the
saddle. It was all over before he quite knew what was
happening; before his body had bounced the second time,
he was dead of a broken neck.

However, the dead man had let out a yelp of fear just a
moment before the noose had tightened around his neck.
One of the two men riding ahead had heard it. He twisted
in the saddle, but could see nothing; the trail bent to the
right just beyond where the ambush had taken place, and
was screened by foliage. "Hold up, Tom," he called out
to the man riding ahead of him. "Somethin's happened to
Pete."

Tom pulled his horse around. "Don't tell me that clumsy
bastard's done gone an' fell off his horse."

"I dunno. I heard him shout."

They rode back down the leaf-shadowed trail with com-
mendable caution, then stopped their horses abruptly when
they saw Pete swinging slowly back and forth, his heels
only a few inches from the ground, his neck grotesquely
stretched. "Jee-zuzz!" Tom hissed.

After a moment's shocked hesitation, both men reacted;
they were in bad trouble and they knew it. But their reaction
was not quick enough. Gabe stepped out into the middle of
the trail a few yards behind them, a pistol in each hand.
"Turn and fight, woman killers," he said quietly.

Both men twisted in the saddle, both trying to bring their
rifles around to bear, but two factors slowed them: the length
of their rifle barrels in these confined quarters . . . and the
unexpected sight of a half-naked man in war paint.

In such a tight space, Gabe's pistol gave him greater

mobility. He began firing, sending bullets into the bodies of the two Pinkertons. Tom got off a shot, but it missed by more than a foot. The fight was over in seconds, with both Pinkertons dead or dying before their bodies hit the ground.

Gabe looked down at the two men he'd shot to death, then up at the one whose neck he'd broken. The rage that had earlier consumed him had by now cooled to an icy desire to kill. He'd tried to warn these men, he'd done his best to frighten them off with the nooses he'd planted in their camp. But they had insisted on coming after him, and in so doing, had killed his woman. These were men who killed for money. They were men to be exterminated. So far he'd killed six. He wondered how many were left.

There were five. About ten minutes before Gabe killed Tom and his companions, Rafe's group of three joined up with the two men mounted double. They heard the shooting, and since it was close, they headed straight toward it. They discovered that things were not going well for their side when the lead man almost ran into Pete's dangling body. "Christ!" the man burst out, fighting to control his startled horse.

Tom and the third man were lying dead just a few yards away. "Close up, boys," Rafe ordered his four men. "Everybody's gonna have to cover everybody else's back."

Their spirits rose a little when they found two of the dead men's horses. Now none of them would have to ride double. Rafe made them push on hard, heading toward the place where they'd heard the original shooting.

They found the man Gabe had chased and killed about two miles up the trail. Some of the men wanted to stop, but Rafe forced them onward. Every man was loaded down with dread by the time they found the last two bodies. "Gawd," one of the men murmured. "We're the on'y fuckin' ones left."

"Uh-uh," Rafe corrected. "Conrad's still out there, somewhere. An' we're gonna get the bastard."

But how? Where was he? The silence of the mountains was everywhere about them. The tracks around the killing grounds had been badly churned up. How to follow? And did they want to? An almost superstitious dread was infecting the men of the posse. Each one of them remembered the terrible cry they'd heard after their quarry had ridden off with his wounded companion. Rafe remembered it, too, and he also felt the dread, but he steeled his will to fight back against it. He, too, was a hunter of men, and he'd never yet come back without the man he was after.

He realized that there was not much more he could do today. It was late in the afternoon. The light was fading. "We'll make camp," he told his demoralized posse, what was left of it. "We'll keep tight security, with most of us awake, and only a couple of men sleeping at any one time. If the bastard tries for us, we'll blow him apart."

Camp was made. There was a wealth of horses now, and Rafe made sure that all were securely within the campsite. He wanted no repeats of that earlier debacle, when Conrad had run off his mounts.

The camp settled down. The fire seemed to make the men feel better, as if it would be able to ward off some nameless evil lurking outside the confines of the camp. Rafe would make certain that the fire was completely out by the time darkness came. He wanted none of his men silhouetted against its light.

Rafe looked around the camp. One man was making coffee. Another was breaking out cans of beans. Another was checking his rifle.

One too few men! There should have been four! "Where's Jeff?" he demanded.

"Oh," one of the men said casually. "He went off somewhere to take a leak. Back in them bushes."

"Why, the stupid—"

They heard the scream before any of them could make a move toward where Jeff had disappeared. It was a horrible scream, blended of terror and pain. Rafe pulled out his pistol and sprinted for the brush. "Come on!" he shouted to the others.

They ran after him, partly so that they would not be left behind. They found Jeff lying on his back, on the ground just within a thicket, with a deep knife wound in his chest.

The dead man's face was twisted into a terrible rictus of fear and agony, as if he'd been looking into the depths of hell itself when he died.

Tracks led away into the underbrush. "That dirty bastard!" one of the men screamed. He started to follow the tracks.

"No!" Rafe snapped, seizing the man by the arm. "That's what he wants us to do . . . go after him on his own ground so he can pick us off one by one. If we want to make it out of here alive, we gotta stick together."

That was the first open admission that they were no longer the hunters, but were now the hunted. It was quickly growing dark. The four survivors nearly ran back to their camp, where they hunkered down on the ground back to back, facing outward toward the hostile darkness. Not a man slept.

Gabe, standing at the edge of the brush about forty yards away, could only make out an undefined black mass that could have been men or could have been piled-up saddles. He was tempted to fire at that black mass, but if he was wrong, if it was only a decoy, then they might immediately fire back at his muzzle flashes, and perhaps hit him.

A diversion was necessary. Gabe melted silently into the brush, working his way back to where he had concealed his horse and equipment, as well as a horse that had belonged to one of the men he'd killed earlier. Gabe spent ten minutes talking to the horse soothingly, getting it to trust him. Then, picking up his Winchester, he vaulted onto the horse's back. He'd already unsaddled the animal, so he was riding bareback, which was better than a saddle for what he intended to do.

He walked the horse as quietly as he could until he was close to the campsite. He knew the men hidden there would be able to hear something moving, but they probably would not yet be certain exactly what it was. Or exactly where it was located.

He urged the horse into a faster walk. A dry branch broke under its hooves. Now they had to have heard him. He thought he could make out a mutter of voices coming from the direction of the camp. Now was the time.

"*Haaiiiiiiyah!*" he screamed while at the same time banging the barrel of his rifle against the horse's withers. The horse, startled, immediately bucked, then broke into a run.

Gabe stayed with the horse until it had nearly reached the edge of the brush, about forty yards from the camp, then he slipped off, rolling as he hit the ground, doing his best to make as little noise as possible.

The horse broke into the open, riderless, but in the darkness the Pinkertons did not know that. "There he goes!" one of them screamed as the horse shot past the campsite. Immediately, provided with such a fine, close target, two of the men jumped to their feet, aiming their rifles. "Get the hell down!" Rafe screamed at them.

It was too late. Gabe saw two forms rise up from the dark mass of the ground. He'd painted a splash of white onto the front sight of his rifle to help him aim in the dark. He rapidly fired half a dozen shots, and saw the two forms disappear back into the darkness from which they'd risen. Screams told him that he'd hit at least one of them.

Before the others could pinpoint his location, Gabe faded back into the brush. A moment later several bullets tore up the undergrowth where he'd been standing. He immediately headed back for his horse in case there was a pursuit.

The Pinkertons were in no condition to mount a pursuit. Gabe's night shooting had had even better results than he'd expected. One man had been killed outright, another was badly wounded, shot through the stomach. Rafe, after checking the man's wound as best as he could in the dark, doubted he'd live an hour.

He was right. The man died about an hour before dawn. Which left just Rafe and one other Pinkerton, a man named Jack. "What the hell do we do now?" Jack asked. "Just wait for the bastard to kill us?"

"Uh-uh," Rafe replied. "We do what we shoulda done yesterday, when we found the others already dead. We get the hell outta here."

It hurt him to say it; it hurt even more when, accompanied by the sole survivor of his posse, he quietly led his horse out of camp. He'd never been beaten before, he'd never failed to complete whatever task he'd been hired to do. Conrad, whoever the bastard was, had to be some kind of devil. Rafe promised himself he'd come back, he'd hunt down the son of a bitch, this time with a hundred men behind him.

Gabe had now made his first mistake. Believing that the Pinkertons would continue to huddle inside the camp, he'd moved about a quarter mile away to await first light. When it came, when the eastern sky had lightened enough for him to begin to make out details, he could see no signs of movement at all from inside the camp. Just two still forms stretched out on the ground.

Forgetting caution, discounting the possibility that more men might be hiding in the brush waiting to ambush him, Gabe mounted his horse and rode straight on in. There was no one there but two dead men, with signs that two horses had left the camp only a little while earlier.

Gabe first collected a loose horse, then set out on the trail. The tracks ran straight, heading toward a pass that led down out of the mountains. Gabe decided that the tracks were at least an hour old. Would he be able to make up the time? Maybe. He'd ride his horses to death, if that's what it took.

He rode wildly, pushing his mounts to their utmost, switching from one horse to another every few miles. Within two hours he knew that he was gaining ground; the tracks indicated that the riders were only a couple of miles ahead of him. But his horses were tiring, and two miles might as well be twenty.

Then he remembered that the main trail, which the riders ahead of him had been following faithfully, took a long loop around to the right. By riding straight on, through very rough country, he might be able to head them off.

The spare horse played out half an hour later. Gabe's own horse was nearly exhausted. Only its great courage and stamina kept it going. Gabe had originally chosen the animal because of its promise of endurance, and it had not disappointed him. But it clearly had only a few miles left before it dropped dead.

Then the countryside opened out again, and he could see the main trail, a couple of hundred yards below him. And on the trail were two men riding horses that looked almost as played out as his own.

Gabe pulled his Sharps from its saddle scabbard and swung down from his exhausted horse. This was it. The ground sloped away steeply beneath him, not impassable, but the difficulty of taking a tired horse down onto the main trail would let the two men get even farther ahead. He'd have only this one chance to stop them. And he must. Gabe had little illusions about what would happen to him if Rafe made it back to civilization with tales of the slaughter in the mountains.

Gabe made no attempt at silence. He flopped down onto his belly, starting a small and noisy rock slide that rattled down toward the main trail. Both men turned to look back up at him. "Jesus! It's him!" Jack screamed.

His voice was drowned out by the roar of Gabe's Sharps. It was a fine shot. The man was slammed out of his saddle by the old buffalo gun's huge bullet. He was dead before he hit the ground.

Rafe, after one upward look at the man who'd wiped out an entire Pinkerton posse, bent low over his horse's neck and urged the animal forward. The exhausted horse stumbled once, but, picking up its master's terror, made that terror its own and broke into a shambling run.

Gabe slipped open the breech of his Sharps. Ping! The empty shell ejected. He shoved in another, slammed the breech closed, cocked the hammer, then settled down to aim.

Rafe was riding straight away from him. An easy target, no need to correct for windage. The rifle roared. For a second, nothing seemed to happen, then the bullet struck. Rafe was first slammed against his horse's neck by the impact, then he raised himself up, back arching, hands flying out to the sides. Gabe could hear Rafe's thin, high scream floating upward toward his vantage point. Then Rafe slowly toppled from the saddle.

It took Gabe ten minutes to work his horse down the slope

onto the main trail. He did not mount when he reached level ground, but led his horse along on foot. He passed the first man he'd shot. Dead as a stone. He continued on. He was only about thirty yards from Rafe when he saw one of Rafe's hands move. Gabe immediately readied his rifle.

There was no need to shoot again. Rafe was no longer a threat. He lay on his back, eyes open, fully conscious, but able to move only the fingers of his right hand. Gabe looked down at him. Rafe looked back up. "Slug broke my back," Rafe said. He spoke clearly, but without force. "I'd consider it a favor if you'd finish me off."

Gabe continued to look down at Rafe. "I'll have to think about it," he finally said. "You haven't done me many favors lately."

Rafe's eyes blinked. Even that hurt, but damned if he'd let Gabe know it. "That's true," he replied. "But I'd still appreciate it. Don't want the ants to get me. Or those damned buzzards. Seen 'em pull the eyes right outta a crippled steer while it was still alive."

Despite what this hired killer had done to him, done to Elena, Gabe felt respect for Rafe. He was not whining, nor was he begging for his life. He was a man of courage. But this was not the time for Gabe to let him know how he felt. "I'll make you a deal," he said. "You tell me who it was that hired you, and I'll give you a quick death."

Rafe hesitated only a moment. "Hell," he finally said. "I don't owe that greasy little fucker a thing. His name's Devane. From Santa Fe."

"Devane?"

"Yeah. But he's gonna disappoint you. He's just a fuckin' business agent, a slippery little lawyer who empties slop buckets for bigger men. But Devane is the one who hired us, and the one who paid out the money. For what good it'll do you."

Gabe nodded. "That's all you know?"

"That's all I know."

"And that's who you ride out to kill women for? A man like Devane? A man who's just a hireling, like yourself?"

Rafe's eyes closed for a moment. When he opened them,

he looked straight at Gabe. "I'm sorry about the woman. She just got in the way."

Gabe felt a moment of rage. He wanted to shoot Rafe in the gut, or leave him to be eaten alive by vultures, coyotes, or insects. But the man had been honest with him. And he showed courage. "I'll give you a moment to look at the sky, the mountains," Gabe said. "Enough time to sing your—"

Then he remembered that white men did not sing death songs. And Rafe did not look like the kind of man who'd fall back on prayer.

"What the hell you talkin' about?" Rafe asked, puzzled. Then Gabe shot him through the heart. The impact of the bullet, and Rafe's muscular reaction, lifted his body several inches off the ground. Rafe's eyes stayed locked on Gabe's face for an instant, then he died, and as the last light faded from his eyes, Gabe thought he saw a flicker of gratitude.

He turned away. This was not over yet. Far from it. There remained a man named Devane. And beyond Devane, how many more?

CHAPTER NINETEEN

Amos Devane was not a man of action, he was not a man who took risks. He was not an initiator, he created nothing, good or bad. Devane had been aware of his limitations since boyhood and had decided quite early in life to make his living, jackal like, off the scraps left behind by more courageous predators. In short, he became a lawyer and an agent.

Devane had done well. He had not made a great fortune, like the men who employed him, but neither had he taken the risks they'd taken. He'd seen many fall along the way, ruined by the daring of their own rapaciousness. Not Amos Devane. The growth of his own modest fortune had been slower but ever so much more steady. Particularly since he'd had the inspiration to come out to the West, where, while the pickings might be more scattered, there were fewer scavengers to fight over what there was.

Several years earlier, Devane had correctly forecast that the level of corruption in the remote territory of New Mexico would give him opportunities not available in the more settled East. He'd been more right than he'd imagined. There was all that land held, titles clouded, by a vanquished people, and everyone knew that the victor was supposed to get the spoils. Devane calculated that even the crumbs from such wholesale robbery would make him a tidy profit.

He'd been right. Devane now owned one of the better houses in the territorial capital of Santa Fe. There was money in the bank, there was plenty of gold set aside, and there were various landholdings, small but choice. As long as his efforts continued to satisfy the truly wealthy, the utterly ruthless men who controlled the land and industry of the United States, Devane would prosper.

Sometimes the activities he was called on to perform exhilarated him, gave him a vicarious participation in the seamier activities of this violent land. He'd felt such an exhilaration when he'd hired Rafe Jenks to hunt down the man who'd been hurting them on the Los Robles land acquisition. Dealing with men like Jenks both thrilled and horrified Devane. An icy killer, Jenks. Devane's flesh had crawled every time Jenks looked in his direction. Eyes like ice water. Devane wondered how many men Jenks had killed.

He'd sent Jenks out days ago. The only reports that had come back to him was that Jenks's posse was having trouble locating his man . . . what was his name? Ah yes. Conrad. Well, it was only a matter of time. Driving Conrad out of the territory would be as satisfactory as having him killed.

Having had a busy day, Devane strolled home from his office. A drab place, Santa Fe, a town made up mostly of low, flat-roofed adobe buildings. Mud houses. Hardly a place you could call a city. Devane was proud of his own contribution to civic improvement, his magnificent house, which he'd had built about half a mile outside the town proper. He could have driven his buggy to and from his office, but he liked the walk, not only to keep himself in good shape, but so that he could have the satisfaction of having his house grow before him bit by bit as he approached.

Ah . . . there it was. First, the two peaked corner towers, then the myriad roofs, and finally, the many windows, doors, and architectural bric-a-brac that made his house so special in this savage land. It would have never occurred to Amos Devane that there were people, civilized people, who might prefer the low, graceful, timeless Spanish architecture of old Santa Fe, with its quiet inner courtyards, hand-painted tiles, and splashing fountains, to his own multi-turreted Victorian monstrosity.

Amos Devane had no such doubts as he approached his house. He knew which kinds of status symbols proclaimed monetary success, and he had one.

He was met at the front door by Señora Maria, his house-keeper, cook, and general slave. Maria was a perpetual cross to Devane; he would have preferred a proper, civilized housekeeper, but such were prohibitively expensive in this distant, isolated, barbarian land. At least he'd taught Maria to stop using those terrible chiles in her cooking. The first meal she'd prepared for Devane had nearly killed him. Now his food was as greasy, bland, and starchy as any that could be had back east.

He dismissed Maria not long after dinner. He'd brought some sensitive papers home with him that he wanted to study, and he never worked on delicate subjects when there was a chance that someone might be looking over his shoulder.

Alone in the house, Devane worked until nearly midnight. He did not mind the late hours at all. This latest commission should bring him a healthy fee, and Devane was ready to work day and night as long as it earned him the money he craved.

When he went to bed that night, Amos Devane felt rather smug. Another couple of years of this, and he would be able to retire. He'd return to civilization with his western earnings and live like the gentleman he knew himself to be.

The smugness was noticeably lacking when he awoke the next morning. Awoke to find a man's face situated not more than a foot from his own, a terrible face, with eyes of such a remarkable coldness and ferocity that even Rafe Jenks's icy eyes seemed kind and warm in comparison. "Wha . . . Who . . . ?" Devane stammered.

"Shut up, or I'll cut your throat," the face said.

Cut . . . his throat? Devane became aware of a coldness beneath his chin. His eyes swiveled downward. He could see the handle and part of the blade of an enormous, evil-looking knife. A horribly sharp knife. He could feel the sting of its edge cutting into the soft flesh of his throat.

"I want to find out why you sent those men after me," the face said.

"M-men?" Devane stammered. "What men?"

"Pinkertons. One of them was called Rafe. My name's Conrad. Gabe Conrad."

Devane found that he was unable to say a thing. Eyes bulging, he studied the man he'd thought would either be dead by now, or long gone. With an effort, he looked away from those terrible eyes, and saw a lean face, framed by shoulder-length, sandy-colored hair. "I'm waiting!" Gabe snapped.

Devane found himself looking into those terrible eyes again. Eyes colored so light a gray that they seemed almost without color. And totally devoid of normal human feeling, which, to Devane, meant any weaknesses that he might manipulate. Those eyes were demanding that he say something. "I . . . I was told to hire them," he stammered.

"You work for the Pinkerton Agency?" Gabe demanded.

When Devane replied, he was practically babbling. "Well . . . they weren't actually Pinkertons. Not for this particular job. Jenks works for the Pinkertons from time to time, but I hired him as an independent contractor for this assignment. Along with his men."

Gabe almost sighed with relief. So he wasn't tangling directly with the Pinkerton Agency, after all. Which might help him survive.

Devane broke into this thoughts. "I'll call them off," he whimpered. "I'll tell them to leave you alone."

To Devane's amazement, Gabe smiled. It was not a re-assuring smile. "I'm afraid you're too late," Gabe said.

"I . . . don't understand."

"They're dead," Gabe replied flatly. "I killed them. Every one."

"You . . . you *what*?" Devane burst out. He could not imagine any single individual wiping out a man like Jenks, not even if Jenks had not had all those other men riding with him. But this maniac's eyes did not seem to be lying, and as Devane considered the possibility, his fear of Gabe deepened.

"Rafe, the man you call Jenks," Gabe said, "gave me your name before he died."

"He . . . talked?"

"In exchange for a quick death. At the end, he was begging me to kill him quickly. Now I want another name. The name of the man who ordered you to hire Jenks."

"Why . . . I couldn't . . ."

"Once again . . . in exchange for a quick death . . . like Jenks."

A spasm of terror passed through Devane's body. Could there be any more horrible death than the knife at his throat? Conrad seemed to think so. Now Devane noticed the traces of war paint on Gabe's face. He became aware of the Indianness of him, and, like most easterners, raised on Indian horror stories from dime novels, he shuddered as he thought of the skin being peeled from his body piece by piece. "Jason Broadbent," he blurted.

"Who?"

"Broadbent. Jason Broadbent. He told me to do it. He gave me the money."

From which you no doubt kept a fat commission, Gabe thought. He had not met many men who disgusted him more than this miserable little worm. Devane looked very much like a grub, the kind that lives under the skin of sick rabbits, a rounded, white little grub. A total parasite. A man whose soul was completely barren. A man to whom the green of money was the only green worth admiring. A man who'd rape the world if it brought him profit.

"Is this Jason Broadbent the same man who engineered the theft of the Los Robles land?" Gabe asked.

"How did you know that?" Devane blurted, startled.

Gabe merely smiled enigmatically. "I want you to tell me all about it," he said.

Words came pouring out of Devane, who was hoping that talking might delay the terrible death resting against his throat. He told Gabe about the company that had been set up back east, with Broadbent's interests hidden within a nest of other companies so that business competitors would not know who was behind various land acquisitions. "I'm the only one who's locally visible," Devane said. "I have power of attorney for the corporation."

Gabe thought back to what his grandfather had told him about corporations. "That means that your signature can bind that company, doesn't it?"

"Why, yes . . . of course."

Gabe actually smiled. Devane flinched, wondering if this was the kind of man who smiled as he killed.

"I'll tell you what," Gabe said. "I'll make you a trade."

Devane tensed. A promise of a quick death again?

"If you sign over the Los Robles land to a man I designate, I'll . . . let you live."

"I can't do that!" Devane replied, horrified. "Broadbent would kill me!"

Gabe smiled again. A terrible, cold smile. "He won't kill you quite the way I will," he said. The knife left Devane's throat. Devane breathed a sigh of relief—until he felt the coldness of the blade moving down his body, finally coming to rest between his legs. Devane felt himself shrivel. "Starting down here won't let you die too quickly," Gabe said. "Unless you bleed to death from what I do to you."

Devane shuddered from head to foot. He'd never been able to abide pain. Even the thought of it made him sick to his stomach. "I'll . . . I'll sign anything you want," he whimpered.

Gabe let him up. Devane led the way into the office near the rear of the house. He was aware of how Gabe towered over him. Even then he still might have tried to bluff it out . . . if it had not been for Gabe's eyes.

Devane drew up a contract of sale for the various parcels that made up the old Los Robles land grant. Gabe watched over his shoulder. "For every mistake you make," Gabe promised, "I'll cut off a finger."

It was said so casually that Devane knew he meant it. Obviously, this wild man had garnered a little legal knowledge somewhere, so Devane was careful to make the document as airtight as possible. When he'd finished, Gabe studied the document carefully, then nodded his satisfaction. "This'll do."

"Fine. Fine. You have what you want, so now you can go."

Again, that cold smile. "Did I say I was going?"

"You . . . you promised. You said you wouldn't kill me if I—"

"I killed Jenks," Gabe replied softly, "because he killed my woman, a young girl from Los Robles. You sent him out to kill that girl."

"Oh . . . Oh, God . . . you can't . . ."

Gabe watched Devane groveling in front of him. Instinct said to kill him, squash him like some noxious insect. But on the other hand, there might be other, much more imaginative punishments that would hurt a man like Devane even more than death. Besides, if he killed him before the contract of sale was recorded, it would probably invalidate the entire document. "Do you have any money in the local bank?" Gabe asked.

The question was so unexpected that Devane answered without thinking. "Yes. And a strongbox."

"Good. Get dressed. We're going to do some banking."

Oh God, he's going to steal my money, Devane thought. But he made no complaints. Going to the bank would delay anything that Conrad might be planning to do to him. And once out in the street, there would be more chance of saving the situation.

Devane dressed, watched closely by Gabe, although he doubted Devane had the guts to reach for a hidden weapon. Gabe picked up one of Devane's hats, put it on, and tucked his hair up underneath the crown, out of sight. After he'd killed Rafe, he'd gone back to where he'd left his gear, next to Elena's burial platform. He was now wearing the best clothes he had. With his duster worn over the clothes, plus Devane's expensive hat, he should be able to pass himself off as a rustic businessman.

He and Devane left the house and headed toward the bank. Gabe stuck close to Devane. "If you call out for help or attract attention in any way," he told the sweating little man, "I'll gut you. My hand will be on the knife every moment. Remember . . . I have nothing to lose by killing you.''

The bank manager was a little confused as Devane, accompanied by a companion, closed his account, then cleaned out his strongbox, but there was not much he could do about it. ''Are you dissatisfied with our service, Mr. Devane?'' he asked plaintively.

''No . . . no, it's all been fine,'' Devane mumbled, aware of Gabe's proximity, of this insane killer's eyes boring into him. ''I just need some cash and some other guarantees for a transaction that must be completed today.''

Wanting to cut his tongue out, aching to scream for help, Devane stuffed the bulk of his worldly wealth into a big gladstone bag, then headed back toward his house, with Gabe walking close by his side. Once inside the house, Gabe opened the gladstone. ''Securities,'' he said. ''Cash. A lot of it, Devane. A man could live very well on this kind of money.''

Devane said nothing. So this man was only a common bandit, after all.

''Don't you think it's cold in here?'' Gabe asked.

The unexpectedness of the question startled Devane. ''I . . . Not really.'' But he shivered anyhow, more from nerves than from actual cold.

Gabe smiled again. Devane had learned to fear those smiles. ''I think we need a fire, Mr. Devane.''

Gabe pushed Devane toward the fireplace. With growing horror, Devane listened to Gabe order him to start a fire . . . using his money and securities as kindling. ''No'' he blurted.

Gabe's face twisted with rage, partly staged, but Devane had no way of knowing that. Suddenly his arm was being twisted, his hand forced down onto a table top. That huge knife was in Conrad's hand again. ''First the little finger,'' Gabe snarled. ''Then the rest, one by one.''

''I'll do it! I'll do it!'' Devane shrieked. Trembling, he began stuffing papers into the fireplace. Bearer bonds. Unassigned stocks. Deeds. Bundles of bank notes. Gabe made him strike the match that started it all burning. Devane stood, watching, tears running down his face as all that lovely wealth, the fruit of years of bowing and scraping to men like Jason Broadbent, went up in smoke.

Amos Devane was a totally broken man by the time Gabe took him to the train station. Gabe handed him five hundred dollars in gold, saved from the fire. ''This will keep you going for a while. And you'd better keep right on going. I'll give you a five-day start, Devane. Then I'm coming after you. And when I catch up . . .''

Devane nodded dully. Terror would follow later, the fear of waking up some morning to feel, once again, cold steel against his throat. The fear of waking up to those remorseless eyes. They would never leave him as long as he lived.

Ten minutes later, Gabe watched the train containing Amos Devane disappear into the distance. How much simpler it would have been to simply kill that miserable little man. But with the papers Devane had signed, he now had a means of evening a score against another man, a man who, before today, he had not even known existed; Jason Broadbent, the man who'd set in motion the train of events that had robbed the people of Los Robles of their land. Events that had ended in the death of a sweet and gentle daughter of that same village. The time was now ripe to make Jason Broadbent pay for the damage and suffering that his greed had brought to innocent people.

CHAPTER TWENTY

Gabe was sitting on a bench in the sun in Santa Fe's central plaza when he saw the old man ride in from a side street, accompanied by three men. He stood up and went out to meet them.

Don Javier stopped his horse a few feet away. He swung down from the saddle and came toward Gabe. "I got your message yesterday. We came as quickly as we could."

Gabe looked at the men behind Don Javier. They were all from Los Robles. "I expected you to bring more men."

"We are all that the village can spare . . . if there's trouble. I . . . Elena's horse returned two days ago. There was blood . . ."

"Elena won't be coming back," Gabe said bleakly.

"How did it . . . ?"

"Twelve men paid for her life with their own. She's lying . . . where she would want to lie."

Don Javier was tempted to ask further questions, but the bleakness of Gabe's expression, the flatness of his voice, warned him not to poke at barely healed scabs.

Gabe handed Don Javier several sheets of paper. Don Javier took them without a word, scanned the pages, casually at first, then his eyes widened. "Why . . . ," he burst out. "Where did you get this?"

"It's all quite legal . . . a bill of sale transferring the original Los Robles land grant holding to you personally . . . as a trustee for the village."

"You say it's legal?"

"It is as soon as you register it at the land commission office."

Don Javier shook his head sadly. "They'll just have another 'accidental' archives fire."

"Let them. When we register these papers, we'll insist on notarized true copies. Something that you can keep in a safe place."

"I . . . Gabriel," the old man said, obviously overcome with emotion. "I don't know how you did this, but—"

"Don't ask. Now let's get over to the land commissioner's office and record the contract."

Don Javier signaled to his three companions. He, Gabe, and the three men crossed the plaza, heading for the commission office. "I wish we had more men," Gabe said again.

"You expect trouble?"

"Maybe. If we can get it over with quickly, maybe not. A certain man will be very upset when he hears about this. It'd be better if we were miles away by then."

They were lucky; the land commissioner was in. In the New Mexico Territory, the office of the land commission had tremendous power. The corrupt Washington appointees who ran the territory regularly used the commissioner to assist with their land frauds, always careful, of course, to make certain that the commissioner got his cut.

To Gabe, the commissioner was a somewhat larger version of Amos Devane, a fat man with small, greedy eyes. He looked up as Gabe's group came into the office, his eyes growing even smaller as he noticed that the men with Gabe were Latins. "Yes?" he said, his voice already combative even before any of the others had said a word.

Gabe thrust the contract of sale into the commissioner's hands. "Record this," he said curtly.

The commissioner took the papers and began to read. By the time he'd reached the second page, his eyes were widening. "Why . . . this is the Los Robles tract!" he burst out.

"You read well," Gabe replied. "Now look at the signature. It's Amos Devane's. A copy of his power of attorney is attached. Record the papers."

"Devane would never have done a thing like this. The land belongs to . . ."

Gabe raised his eyebrows. So this fat pig was in on Broadbent's swindle. "Record them," he repeated, "or, by God, I'll kill you."

The commissioner swallowed hard. "Look here, whatever your name is! You can't come in here and threaten . . ."

Gabe leaned toward the other man, his eyes cold. "The name's Conrad. Gabe Conrad."

The commissioner's eyes widened. "Conrad?" he said weakly. "The man who . . . ?"

"Record those papers," Gabe repeated one more time, his icy gaze trapping the commissioner's eyes.

The commissioner lurched to his feet, clutching the papers. "Of course," he murmured. "Whatever you say, Mr. Conrad."

He bustled over to a large open book, the kind used to record legal documents. Before making any entries, he called to a clerk to bring him a pen and the official stamp. The clerk, who had heard what Gabe had said to the commissioner, appeared to be quite nervous as he brought over the items his employer had requested. Gabe saw the commissioner saying something to the clerk, although he could not quite make out the words. Probably trying to calm him down.

The clerk headed back toward his desk. Gabe walked over to watch the commissioner make entries in the ledger. Looking over the man's shoulder, he saw that he was apparently doing everything correctly.

"Gabriel!"

It was Don Javier's voice. Gabe turned. "The clerk," Don Javier said. "He's slipped out a side door."

"Damn!" Gabe snapped. He spun back to face the commissioner, who was grinning triumphantly. "What did you say to him?" Gabe demanded.

The grin faded. "Why . . . nothing. He . . . just went out for his lunch."

"At ten in the morning?"

The commissioner shrugged. He still looked afraid, but

he also looked as if he knew that help was on the way. Gabe pushed past him and checked the ledger. The entry seemed to be complete. Gabe took back the contract of sale and waved it in the commissioner's face. "We want a true copy made of these documents."

"Why . . . of course. Perhaps after lunch, when my clerk returns . . ."

A terrible iciness settled over Gabe. "If we don't have that true copy within fifteen minutes, you greasy little man, I'll blow your heart out."

The commissioner found himself unable to look away from Gabe's eyes. He had been afraid before, but now he was terrified. He saw his death in those eyes. "Yes," he mumbled. "Right away. I'll do it myself."

Gabe stood over the commissioner as he sat at a desk and began to copy out the documents. Don Javier's three men stood guard at the doors and windows. Don Javier was called forward to sign. Finally it was done. Don Javier took the papers and put them away inside his coat. "Let's go," Gabe said.

But it was already too late. As he and the four Los Robles men stepped out of the land office, five men were heading toward them.

It was Jason Broadbent, accompanied by four obvious gunslingers. They still might have made it; Broadbent did not know who they were, although Gabe had spent most of the previous day observing Broadbent, but the land commissioner came running out of his office behind them. "Those are the men, Jason," he shouted. "They've got some phony contract of sale!"

"Thanks for the warning, Ben," Broadbent replied.

"Somebody oughta go and find Amos," the commissioner continued. "He can clear up this mess."

Broadbent turned an unsmiling face toward the commissioner. "Devane left town yesterday afternoon," he said coldly. "After cleaning out his bank account." He jerked his chin in Gabe's direction. "I understand that this gentleman saw him off at the train station."

"My God," the commissioner murmured. "Amos sold you out, Jason."

"Looks like it. But you and I can clear up any legal misunderstandings, can't we, Ben?"

"Sure, Jason . . . sure."

Obviously, a ledger page was going to turn up "lost." Then the commissioner remembered what he had just been forced to do. "They have a notarized copy of the contract of sale, Jason."

"Who does?"

"The old man."

Broadbent turned to face Don Javier. "Is that so, Pancho?" he asked.

"It is so, *señor*," Don Javier replied.

"You know, Pancho, you could be accused of being involved in a land fraud. Use some sense. Hand over the papers and we'll forget the whole thing."

"*Señor*," Don Javier said softly. "It is you who have tried to defraud my people. You are a thief and a pig. The papers stay with me."

Jason Broadbent was a big man; tall, fairly well put together, with a neatly trimmed beard and regular features. Yet, there was about him an air of a man who was missing something, a man who was not quite complete. Of course, Gabe realized. He has no soul . . . other than money.

Broadbent and Don Javier stood facing one another, Don Javier physically smaller and much older, but straight and strong, exuding infinitely more dignity than Jason Broadbent. "One more chance, Pancho," Broadbent said, his voice ugly.

Knowing that a fight was imminent, Gabe had already begun to shift to the right, so that he would be able to cover all four of Broadbent's gunslingers. The three Los Robles men were doing the same, but shifting to the left so that they could cover Broadbent's men from the other side.

"Come on, greaser," Broadbent snarled, taking a step toward Don Javier. "I'm not a patient man."

"You may go to hell, *señor*," Don Javier said quietly.

Gabe saw Broadbent's face darken with rage. He looked back over his shoulder, toward his men. "Gun 'em down, boys!" he shouted.

Many hands reached for weapons, but Gabe, reading Broadbent's intent, had gone for both his pistols before Broadbent's gunmen had even started to move. It was his guns, blasting lead toward the gunslingers, that diverted their attention long enough so that the Los Robles men were able to open up on them from the other side.

Caught between two fires, unable to settle on any one target, the gunmen fell subject to a fatal panic. Two went down at once. Another lived long enough to take a few steps to the rear, then he, too, went down, riddled by bullets. The remaining gunman took to his heels and ran for his life.

Gabe had already twisted back toward Don Javier. There was no need. Broadbent was clawing under his coat for a pistol, but so was Don Javier. Gabe saw the old man pull an enormous old .44-caliber Colt Dragoon cap-and-ball pistol from his waistband. Broadbent actually shot first. The bullet from his little .32-caliber popgun tore half the lapel from Don Javier's coat.

Then Don Javier fired. The big soft lead bullet took Broadbent low on the left side, half doubling him up. Don Javier stepped forward, firing again, his second bullet hitting Broadbent high up on the right side of his chest.

The impact slammed Broadbent back against a hitching rack. He staggered, caught his balance, then tried to bring up his little pistol, but Don Javier was still walking toward him remorselessly. Gabe heard the big hammer of the old horse pistol crank back into full cock. "For the people of Los Robles," Don Javier cried out. "For Elena!"

His third shot took Broadbent in the pit of the stomach. Broadbent folded in half, then fell on his face. Don Javier walked up to his opponent's prone body and turned him over with his foot. Broadbent stared up at Don Javier, his mouth working soundlessly, frothy blood bubbling from between his lips.

Don Javier was starting to cock the pistol a fourth time. Gabe walked over and put his hand on the gun. "Let him choke on his own blood," he told the old man.

Don Javier had been staring down at his fallen enemy.
Now he shook his head, and the killing light went out of
his eyes. "You're right, Gabriel. He's not worth the price
of another bullet."

Jason Broadbent died as they were mounting their horses.
Gabe looked back to see a crowd forming around the bodies
that littered the street. There had been witnesses to the fight,
many of them Latins. It was a clear case of self-defense. It
might be a good idea for Don Javier to stay in Los Robles
for a while, but there should be no legal problems.

They rode for several miles without saying anything.
Finally, Gabe pulled his horse to a stop. The others stopped,
too, looking around quickly to see if Gabe might have spotted danger, perhaps an attack.

There was nothing. Gabe held out his hand to Don Javier.
"I believe you say . . . *adiós*."

Don Javier held out his hand in return. His face showed
little surprise. "You are leaving, then."

"Yes."

"You sadden us. We would like you to stay."

Gabe shook his head. "It would . . . hurt."

Don Javier nodded. "Ah yes . . . I know the feeling. But
you must remember, my friend . . . you will always be welcome in Los Robles."

Both Gabe and Don Javier had too much dignity to pro-
long the farewell. Gabe shook hands with the other three
men, then turned his horse and kicked it into a fast trot.
When he'd reached a small ridge about a quarter of a mile
away, he stopped the horse and looked back. Don Javier
had stopped his horse, too. Gabe saw the old man wave to
him. He waved back.

Then, turning his horse toward the north, Gabe prepared
to ride out of New Mexico, even more alone than when
he'd ridden in.